The Blood Makes It Real

Mark Lopez

Visit my website MarkLopezAuthor.com

Find me on Twitter **@Darkmarklolo**

On Facebook @DarkMarkLoloAuthor

I.

I squeezed his neck a little bit harder now, turning the whites of his eyes bloodshot as they ran into the back of his head. A yellow hue was slowly edging in from the outsides of his eyeballs towards the brown surrounding his wide dark pupils. I could feel his muscles involuntarily spasm as his body seized and shook while he slowly ran out of oxygen.

The sad truth for him now though, was there was no amount of twitching… that would allow his lungs to ever again take in so much as one more breath. His body convulsed for a full minute, the shades of his face changing in odd patterns looking a bit like a slow moving kaleidoscope.

I looked down at him, taking in what was in front of me. His once dark and healthy looking skin had taken on a much paler hue which was now bordering the color purple, almost black in the dim light of this desolate hotel room.

I had picked this place because it was in the middle of nowhere. You could go out to the road and look in any direction and wouldn't see another sort of establishment for miles. It really wasn't much to look at, just a cheap $35 a night hellhole for traveling tourists and people who probably wouldn't stop unless they were desperate for a place to stay.

The carpeting was straight out of the 70's. It was a hideous shade of red that had probably covered up its fair share of messy nights long before I came along. The table that held the television was topped with the same material they try to pass off in cheap trailer homes as fire retardant countertop. Rather than painting the walls white, they opted to put up wallpaper that seemed straight out of a Tim Burton movie. It probably started out white, but no doubt the amount of cigarettes over the years that had been smoked in the room had changed it into more of a mustard brown. Even that hadn't held up well over the years and was peeling back randomly throughout the room.

His feet were the last parts of him to stop twitching. His tongue hanging out of his mouth just the slightest bit looked almost rubbery and seemed to have stiffened up already. The last thing he heard was my low, excited breathing as I stared into his white eyes as his life slowly slipped away.

I like to stare into the eyes of my victims as they die if I get a chance. I'm not really sure what it is that I expect to see exactly but it intrigues me. I guess I'm looking for some proof of life beyond death where I have no doubt many enemies waiting for me. Sometimes I think I see something fade out, some kind of light or energy, some might even say it was the soul leaving the body.

I would rather face a militia of my victims in the afterlife, than just fade out when my body dies. That in itself keeps me looking. The last few times I had killed I have felt more than saw something actually leaving their bodies. It usually happened just a few moments after my victims actually lost consciousness. Their eyes will glaze over and then as if someone flipped a switch, they seem to go out completely.

I looked down at my new freshly squeezed middle aged Mexican, laying there with shock and bewilderment on his face relaxing into the last look he would ever make. I could see the darkening in his pants where his bowels let loose as his body lost control. I wasn't happy about having to clean that mess up but it was well worth it.

I couldn't help but smile to myself. I wasn't after all at a place where I could be connected to anything other than possibly witnesses seeing me leave. I had kept this all as quiet as I could and would be just another nameless face leaving one of the rooms like any other day. As long as I didn't leave any obvious signs of struggle or mess nobody would ever know any different. Besides, the room was paid for until tomorrow around noon and nobody seemed to notice the noise the Mexican had made coming into the room.

I looked over the length of his body and didn't doubt that he had exercised this morning. He had one of those physiques most men would appreciate having themselves. He was lean, muscular and well-proportioned. The thick mass of muscle on his neck alone wouldn't have been natural without a decent workout schedule. There were also lots of prominent veins bulging in all the right places adding to the athletic fit image he obviously liked to portray.

It was almost a shame I had to cut him up. Time was wasting though so I figured I'd better get to it. It would be about 3:30 am by the time I was done, the sun would be coming up shortly after that so I wanted to be done and gone before then.

I was getting pretty good at the art of butchery now. First, I grabbed the front of his loose fitting fake silk shirt and I ripped the buttons open revealing his slowly cooling chest. I had to lift his body up a little bit in order to get his handcuffs off his wrists so I could take his arms out of his sleeves and his shirt all the way off. I threw the shirt over to the side of the room and did the same with his pants. He was sprawled out on the floor below me in his underwear which I had left on him. I couldn't help but lick my lips looking down at his physique.

The anticipation was driving me crazy. I grabbed a length of rope from my bag and tied a piece to each foot about 9 inches apart and then reached down and scooped him up putting one arm under his upper back and the other under his knees and carried him into the bathroom. The hotel rooms shower head was solid enough to hold his weight luckily because I didn't really think about that before I had decided that this would be a good place for tonight's business. I also hadn't counted on unexpected guests tonight, especially well built decent sized ones.

For my own shower, I had gone to my local hardware store and bought some metal bracing so I could do things of this nature without breaking the shower head from the wall. I had to step over the body of Trina, a blonde prostitute who had gotten this room in her name after a little story about my having warrants, as an excuse not to put my name anywhere near the place. Sure, I had paid the cash for the room, but it was in her name, so I could afford to be a bit… messy if I needed to be.

I walked past the motels rock hard bed in this cheap ass room. It was that dirty lumpy rectangle of a mess nobody wanted to sleep on with the comforters nobody had seen in a store since the early 70's. The bed smelled of stale cigarette smoke and random body odors as if they hadn't changed them since the place opened. It was the kind of bed that you wouldn't see in a room over 35 bucks a night and at the moment it was occupied by the recently deceased body of Violet, a hooker I had indirectly killed earlier tonight. I can't truly claim that death if I'm being perfectly honest, that one was more like… fate.

I walked past her and the Mexican into the bathroom at the end of the short hallway. I looked down into the bathtub into the wide eyed but now dull look of my latest kill Trina before the Mexican pimp had showed up at the door. She was still so pretty, the look of terror she had died with had also relaxed on her face. She still had my large, 9 inch long serrated knife I had used earlier to impale her in her chest to help ease her pain. After all, I'm not a complete monster.

I decided to dismember the big guy first since he would be the most time consuming and take up the most space. I removed Trina and put his body into the shower stringing him up with the rope tying his feet together. I took the knife out of her gorgeous chest and turned and sawed into the side of the dead pimp's neck. The process was similar to the slitting of a slaughtered cows neck so they can be drained of their blood making for a much less messy dismemberment. This time the "cow" was already dead and didn't exactly have a beating heart to help ease the blood out of him so I took great care to not only sever the jugular and allow the maximum amount of blood to leave his still warm body, but I also slit him from ear to ear. His head was beginning to bloat up from the blood pooling in it. I filled up an old mason jar I brought with me with as much of the blood as I could catch running from his open neck to use for later.

I was surprised at the amount of blood that drained into the tub even after I thought there couldn't possibly be any more. The lack of blood in his empty body was turning his now pale skin an almost albino hue. When I was satisfied with the amount of blood that had drained from him and expected no more, I picked up my knife and continued to saw on his neck, separating layer by layer of meat from meat, until I finally got to his spinal column at which the knife stopped sawing smoothly. I applied the dull side of the blade to the back of his neck carefully bracing it to prevent slipping and cutting myself when I hit the sturdy handle hard with my right hand. The blow broke the bones of his neck with a clean snap, assuring me that I wouldn't dull my knife sawing off the rest of his head.

This I would put into a plastic bag by itself, so I could take it with me without blood getting on anything. This hotel room happened to have a few extra trash bags in the little garbage pails they put in every room, giving me more space to put his body parts in. I brought some bags with me but I didn't count on the extra bodies today. Now with the head in the first bag, next came the rest of the body so I could begin on the next one. I took their clothes and personal things that they had on them and stuffed them into a separate trash bag and took a shower to rinse off the blood. When I was satisfied that I hadn't left any fingerprints or other obvious evidence behind I threw the bags in my trunk and drove us all home.

II.

Home sweet home…

I drove up to the house hitting the button on my visor so I could pull into my dingy but yet spacious garage. I walked inside my house unlocking my squeaky door; taking note that I needed to grease the hinges. It took me a couple of trips in order to get the dozen or so bags with all the various body parts. I put the three bags with the heads in them on my faded kitchen counter and the rest in my refrigerator for now to keep them fresh. I took the heads out of their bags and put them into my sink to wait until it was their turn to be worked.

I wasn't expecting any company as it was so late. Even if someone were to stop by I wouldn't be letting them in so I wasn't worried about being too discreet. I liked to keep to myself and in all the years that I had lived here I had confidence that I would have little to no unexpected visitors. I had darkening curtains hung all around the house blocking anyone from being able to look inside as well, for obvious reasons.

I pulled out my deep, five gallon cooking pot from the cabinet beneath the counter and filled it with water with the sprayer from the sink as there was no room with all the heads inside of it. Their faces hadn't changed much, besides what had been done by the mechanics of sawing the heads off but they still looked surprised to be looking up at me from my sink about to boil the flesh off of their skulls.

I turned on the stove, making sure to turn the dial back after it lit to stop the clicking from the ignitor and added some salt to get the water boiling faster. I also poured in a little bit of coconut oil to help facilitate the separation of flesh from bone and to prevent anything from sticking to the bottom of the pot.

I took out the head of the pimp and put it into the boiling water setting my timer for about 45 minutes. I wanted to bring it to a boil but not overbearingly so it would spill out of the pot so I just set the flame to a medium high strength. I wanted to loosen up the skin and flesh from the bones so I wouldn't have so much work to do with them later. The water reached a nice low boil I found over time was the perfect time to put a head in. Almost instantly it started turning darker than before. Instead of being pale their faces would become more of an almost pink hue.

Sometimes when I looked at them with their faces bobbing in the boiling water I would have to wonder if the heat somehow would kick start their brain even if only for a moment and they could actually see a view of themselves from inside the pot. Kind of like what the view from under water in a hot tub might be.

Boiling them was going to cause the bloody and weaker parts of flesh to turn more solid which in turn would soften the bond between bone and muscle along the harder to pull off spots of their skulls such as the scalp and the jaw behind the ears.

While the head was boiling I made use of the time slicing up the sections of the dead pimps' body that I had put into the refrigerator. I took his thighs and sliced down the length of them cutting away the meat from the bone the best I could before slicing the pieces into less recognizable sections of meat. I wasn't worried someone would see them but I still wanted to avoid the: "Just in case" factor. Just in case I overlooked something one time, there would be less chance that something so obvious as a recognizable cut up body in my freezer would create problems for me. I just feel that it's better to have my bases covered.

I let his head sit a few extra minutes while I finished up the task of slicing his left thigh into smaller pieces. Slicing up the body parts was actually pretty easy with my new knife set I bought off of a late night infomercial, they promised that it would cut through leather and bone and even most metals as he demonstrated on various cans of soda and even one can of ravioli. What really sold me was how easily it could slice through a tough raw steak, so of course I had to try the set. It was a great investment if you ask me. The whole process from beginning to end took a little more than an hour for his entire body.

I turned off the stove so I could change out the water and pulled his head out of it. Most of the flesh was so soft I could just rub it with my finger and it would slide right off. I could feel my saliva glands going crazy, and my stomach agreed with the low growls it was giving me. I was definitely going to have to try this guy tonight but I was going to finish rubbing all the flesh off his skull first so I could dry and treat it so that it wouldn't rot.

That had become a specialty of mine, preserving skulls. I liked to have them around my house. The coating on them was more silicon based and looked more like a rubber so people would probably just assume they were medical and I displayed them as such on a shelf in my garage.

I plucked one of the warm, slightly shrunken but still juicy eyeballs from his socket with the help of a little triangular serrated spoon I bought specifically for this purpose. I put a little bit of spicy Asian sauce on it, and popped it into my mouth. I got chills on the back of my neck as I chewed it up. Freshly cooked eyes are my favorite way to enjoy them. I used to wonder how people would eat things even as simple as fish eyes, now I knew how they did it. It was becoming a delicacy to me, but it didn't start out that way.

When I was still new to killing people, I couldn't imagine doing something like that. The thought of putting anything from a dead human into my mouth made me sick to my stomach. By the time I finally tried my first bite of human flesh I had to get over the initial gag factor that came with it. Much the same as if someone throws up on you. It seems to trigger much the same way and without warning.

After some time it gets to be kind of second nature and sort of stops bothering you any more than it does to put a burger into your mouth that used to be a cow. I also went through the whole emotions of naming an animal and then having to kill it in a different sort of way.

It can be hard to look into the eyes of my victims and see the faces of what would eventually become my food. It was too much for me at first but I overcame it the same way as the ability to pop eyeballs into my mouth, by getting used to it. I could never eat them raw though, that would be like eating a fish without cooking it, and I don't like sushi. It's just unnecessary. Eyeballs are just a little bit too squishy and a bit too slimy for me uncooked; though I did try them raw once. I can't say that I don't have my moments of queasiness though because at times… I still do.

I took the time to slide and peel the flesh off of his head until I had just the nice white skull and nothing else. I mostly used my fingers, but also had to utilize my needle nosed pliers since some of the flesh on the scalp doesn't like to come off as easy as the rest. For the most part, the skin on the head becomes real loose and saggy enabling it to shrink away from the skull a little bit before I even touch it, allowing me to tear and pull most of it away at once.

Sometimes I like to take certain body parts from the people that I've killed. Things such as a finger or an ear, sometimes I might even take a tongue. It depends on how they were acting at the time. For example if they talked a lot of shit to me, which is I must say rare but it does happen; I might take their tongue. If they defiantly stared at me, I might cut out an eye and save that in a glass jar full of embalming fluid like some sort of morbid trophy only a maniac would have. If they refuse to listen to me ignoring what I say, I might cut an ear off to get their attention. It really depends on my mood.

I already had a couple human brains well preserved in my freezer and I wasn't shopping for extra body parts to keep around the house now. It was enough that I already had a miniature body world in the garage, now I would have a couple more skulls to add to my collection. I put them in a little nook of my garage towards the back right corner. It was a little 6 foot by 4 foot area hidden from the rest of the garage by a hanging black sheet that I put up to make it look as if it were more a part of the wall, instead of the truth that it was hiding a little area with real human body parts in it. It was kind of my own little sanctuary where I could smoke a joint in my chair and admire the sacrifices made in the name of madness.

I had about 6 human heads now on a makeshift shelf I had put in the space on the left wall of the nook. On the right side was another shelf about a foot higher with a few jars with random body parts in it. In the middle was my chair and a little table in case I needed to work on something privately. One of the jars had a brown eye and a blue eye in it as well as a swollen half tongue. The other jar had two ears in it and a middle finger I had cut off of one particularly un-terrified boy when I was younger. That started a beautiful night filled with terror for a guy with supposedly no fear. By the time I was done he definitely had one fear... me. I had to keep that one.

I was up to about eight human skulls now including these new two. I would be putting the rest of the jars in the basement when I was finished building the hidden room I had planned. I never bury a body. Too many people get caught trying to dispose of bodies like that. I just eat well for a while, then once the bones dry out they are going to be ground into a fine powder. I could make that powder into an abrasive cleaning agent, or I could just sprinkle it as I drove down the highway and nobody would ever be the wiser.

As I was putting the meat into my deep freezer in my half-finished basement I couldn't help but smile as I remembered the neighborhood barbeque a few of the neighbors started this year and for some reason they decided to invite me. I decided to join them for it. Since the neighbor Yvonne from down the street came over I've been a bit nervous about someone stopping by again. I just politely let her know that I didn't like people to just stop by because I worked from home and couldn't be disturbed while I was working because it involved being on the phone. She seemed satisfied with that at the time and I haven't heard anything else about it.

I do get the friendly neighborly wave when I drive by on my way home that feels just a little bit forced. The neighbors around were under the impression, according to her, that I had something to hide and rumors were already going to the dark side since I was that guy who would always leave from the garage and never really talked to any of the neighbors. A couple of them even whispered that I must have some kind of dark secrets. They had no clue.

Yvonne told me about one of the neighbors in particular, "Miss Betty the gossip queen" as she was known, who had suggested keeping kids away from my house just in case I was into "little boys or girls" or liked to rape women walking by. I laughed at that because I got the sudden image of her being that lonely old neighbor woman who wanted sex but didn't have the luck to actually land anybody, as if that curiosity of hers was nothing more than a fantasy. I was surprised that Yvonne was telling me all of this but she told me as I'm sure she told many others, "You just have one of those faces."

I gotta say though, if I hear that Miss Betty has been spewing her venomous whispers about me again or talks any more shit about me, she might just get her wish for companionship one last time.

III.

It was a pleasant, warm day when my neighbor Yvonne came over for the first time. I heard a knocking at my door and instantly the feeling of panic came over me. Nobody ever stopped by my place. The feeling of panic quietly faded away when I thought about the fact that it could just be a religious zealot trying to sell me on whatever story they were peddling today. I opened the door ready to let them know I wasn't interested and that my *No Solicitors* sign should have let them know that. Instead I was greeted by a portly woman with an all- too-recognizable smile. It was the smile that said, "Hi, I'm a nosy neighbor who doesn't have enough of my own business to keep me satisfied. Can I borrow some of yours?"

"Hi my name is Yvonne." She said. "I'm your neighbor across the street." She reached out her hand towards mine. I shook it weakly. She was about 45 with blond hair that for some reason she had up in an old beehive due. Not quite as high as they wore them then but I had to stifle my initial laughter anyways.

"What can I do for you?" I asked.

That was one of the rare times from that point on that I would actually get to talk. She told me a little about herself. She was, according to her, a 40 year old divorcee. She had a son who was a doctor, who could afford a whole bunch of crap I stopped listening to after a while. It almost seemed that she only cared about what he had accomplished. She didn't even mention his personality, or his likes or dislikes. It made me sad for him. I wasn't about to invite her in so I stepped out on the porch with her and shut the door behind me. I noticed a slight turn of her eyebrow as if she was expecting me to let her in. I ignored it.

She began telling me about the neighbors. She talked about Betty mostly and her incessant gossiping. Almost as if she was jealous of her. She let me know never to tell Betty anything I didn't want everyone else to know. My first thought was that this was good advice all around. I found out that Betty was widowed twice. Yvonne suspected they were both suicides, "Don't tell anyone but Betty once confided in me about destroying her first husband's suicide note in the fireplace cause she was afraid people would think bad of her, but my thought is, why would it be unreasonable to think she could have done the same with the second husbands?"

I smiled awkwardly and wondered what the hell the purpose of her visit was.

"So… what can I do for you?" I asked again.

"Oh sorry!" she said, "I just get to talking and forget what I came over for! Alright well, we're having a neighborhood barbeque and we were wondering if you'd care to join us, get to know us? You have lived here for a while now right?"

"Yeah I've lived here for quite some time now" I didn't really like being asked so many questions but I stayed patient, feeling a bit uncomfortable about the whole idea.

"Well, we're all nice friendly folks, so no need to hide your good looking self like a serial killer or something." At that she blushed and laughed nervously. It was obviously some kind of a test question. I laughed and smiled hoping I was just being paranoid. That was the last thing I needed or wanted with a hobby like mine was to draw weird suspicions from people, especially neighbors. I would have to go to this neighborhood barbeque if I wanted to quell their suspicions. Eventually people would just realize that I wasn't a social kind of neighbor and leave it be. For now though, I had a refrigerator full of human bodies and I needed to make sure that people weren't so curious anymore.

And hell, I did have all kinds of meat.

"I suppose that would be cool… get to know the neighbors. I'm a pretty hermetic person actually; I just keep myself so busy. I would be glad to bring some of the meat I have from my latest hunt too." I felt like I was speaking before thinking at first but I began to really think about it and some perverse part of me wanted to watch other people eating their fellow Earthlings, as I did. I know it sounds twisted, but especially when they wouldn't know that that's what it was they were eating.

Her eyes lit up, "Oh you're a hunter?" She asked with a look of relief on her face. She obviously knew some hunters and felt comfortable around them. "My daddy was a hunter as was my late husband, bless their souls; y'all are a rare breed." She smiled more warmly now. "So what do you hunt?"

I didn't want many more questions about this so I just gave her a general answer. "I like the more exotic meats; sometimes moose meat, sometimes bear, it really just depends on what's out there."

I want her to leave.

I didn't get what I wanted as she continued telling me the neighborhood introductions. I had to restrain myself from rolling my eyes or showing impatience as she went on. I had the huge three story blue house to the right as you drive into the cul-de-sac. I had a neighbor named Steve to the left. He lived in a nice two story tan colored house with a nice lawn he kept looking nice which I appreciated. I took care of my yard best I could when most people were at work so I didn't have to meet them or get to know anyone.

Up to this point I hadn't done more than nod or give a polite smile and wave so I could blend in and nothing more. Behind me was 10 acres of land full of trees that was like my own personal forest. I owned it so didn't have to worry about anything more than a neighbor to the left and one even farther away to the right, and then people living down the road a ways. Steve's home was to the left of mine but it was probably a good few acres of space between us. Both of our homes were built as to allow more area in the back of our places and plenty of solitude.

To my right was another property that belonged to the quiet neighbors, Terry and Victoria. They were avid church goers who never missed a Sunday and gave 15% percent rather than 10 to their church. They were, from the sounds of it your average brainwashed middle income Americans. Yvonne said, "I like them more than most Christians, since they aren't the kind that spews fire and brimstone. They don't say garbage like, 'every little kid whose parents aren't Christian is going to join their parents in hell.'" Maybe she had potential to grow on me after all.

Terry and Victoria had probably an acre of property front and back as did most of the other neighbors around here. Next to the devout Christians was an elderly couple who mostly stayed inside and kept to themselves. They seemed sweet enough according to Yvonne although there was a rumor going around that they were going to die soon. It was widely thought that whichever one died first would likely be joined soon after by the other.

"That is just so romantic, the love between them. I had that once." Yvonne said as she continued on.

At the end on that side was Betty's little yellow cottage style house. She had a quaint little garden with easy to maintain flowers requiring little effort. She liked to be outside a lot in her sundresses and floral nightmares nobody had any business wearing outdoors. She would sit out there for hours drinking her light beer and chain-smoking only acting busy when people were watching or coming over to gossip.

Across from Betty was a young couple one of whom she called the business man, Chris. Chris was always gone and his young, pretty wife Kira was always home waiting on him to be home with her. Nobody around here liked Chris because of the tears that spilt out of Kira's eyes because he was always gone and had excuse after excuse why he 'can't make it home tonight.'

"Granted he was working out of state and country sometimes but he even stayed away when he was here working." Yvonne said.

I felt a little itch when she mentioned him the first time I met Kira. She was a beautiful redhead with striking green eyes and very long eyelashes. She looked like she had literally stepped off of the page of a beauty magazine. It didn't take long to realize that she was naturally beautiful. She seemed truly humble though, not typical of someone as gorgeous as she. I had a sudden urge to torture her husband a little bit for her, and I probably would if it wasn't so close to home.

I wasn't much for shitting where I eat, especially when it didn't involve me. I was comfortable with the way things were right now, nobody really ever bothered me up to this point and I was free to do whatever it was that I needed to do. I had enough money to pay my bills and allow me to live a relatively free lifestyle.

My father died when I was 13 and had managed to make quite a successful business out of a car dealership. After he passed away he left my mother two homes and around half a million dollars. Another $250,000 went to me from his life insurance and he also left me the business. I had no interest in dealing cars and sold it for quite a nice profit. I wouldn't have to worry about money for the rest of my life. He was hit by a car he had sold to a man only a week before. My mother was devastated after my father died and started drinking heavily. She loved me but everything in this place reminded her of my father and she soon wanted nothing to do with it. When I turned 18 she signed this house over to me for $1 and I have been living in it ever since. With my only real bills being utilities on the house, and property taxes once a year, I was living comfortably.

Yvonne finally looked down at her watch as if it had just now occurred to her that time had passed. "Oh my where does the time go? Anyhow the barbeque will be around 6. I had better get on home and get some things ready."

"I'll be there." I assured her with a smile. "Nice meeting you by the way," I said and shook her hand.

"You too!" she said with a genuine smile shaking my hand softly before she walked out the door back to her house. I had some work to do.

IV.

The second time the neighborhood barbeque came along; I was more than excited to go. I was definitely pretty nervous at the first one, but that quickly faded once I saw that by neighborhood barbeque they meant only a few people would be showing up. I doubt this was on purpose as most people only wanted to be left alone. It definitely wasn't from lack of trying on Yvonne and Betty's part.

The first barbeques attendance was only Betty, Yvonne and I. Yvonne and I stayed the longest, while Betty only stayed for about 45 minutes and didn't say much more than her own name as she weakly shook my hand with hers. After that she nearly avoided me completely. I didn't know what to make of it at first but as Yvonne and I spoke more it started becoming a bit clearer because she likes to whisper 'need to knows' when she knows the wrong people weren't paying attention.

I didn't catch the signs initially but as she talked softly to me about Bettie's incessant need for male affection in a low voice so she wouldn't hear her, I kept catching Betty staring at me. I decided to test it and motioned forward with my crotch just as she was mindlessly looking me up and down from afar. As she ate her one and only burger, holding it near the side of her face, I pretended not to notice her wandering eyes. She held her other arm across her stomach, looking slightly insecure. She saw the hip thrust and at that moment licked her lips in a way that said she wanted to do more than clean off some mustard. She saw that I noticed and became embarrassed right away. She looked down as she finished her burger, averting her gaze and shifting from side to side.

I had brought about 8 generous slices of healthy white girl to grill. Neither of them seemed to recognize any difference in the meat and easily assumed they were pork chops. I quickly said "They're thick boneless chops." Before either one of them asked. This seemed to satisfy them both. They each got a nice little steak and sat down. I couldn't help but stare at them while they were eating the human meat. Occasionally I'd catch myself and quickly look away before they noticed.

I had never known this kind of excitement before, until now I hadn't shared this with anyone else. I still wasn't really sharing it with them but something about watching this happen was making my soul tingle in the deepest regions of my being. I could see the glistening on their lips that was only yesterday greasing the inner workings of a neatly disassembled prostitute.

Yvonne said, "I'm a bit sad, I wanted to try some of the hunted meat you were talking about." She gave the slightest pout of her lip, making her look twenty years younger for a second. "But I suppose that was one of the most delicious chops I have ever had… and that is saying something!"

I smiled and said "Next time, I promise." Betty left as quickly as she could get out of there thanking me for the food and heading off mumbling something about a headache. Yvonne and I cleaned up and went home ourselves soon after. She wasn't surprised at the way Betty was acting, or that she had skipped out before any kind of cleaning had to be done. She was only shy at first, and then she opened her legs like she was in a race. I was feeling better about taking a little bit of time away from this craziness that my life had become. I didn't think it was going to be as comfortable as it was but Yvonne isn't so bad so long as I don't offer any information. She liked to talk a lot. That might come in handy someday.

The weather happened to be perfect for tonight's barbeque. Not too breezy or hot, it was just right. I met Yvonne like usual asking to be pointed to the grill. She brought me over to her house so I could grab hers from the back porch. We decided this time to have it by mine and Steve's houses since we had more room for everyone to sit and relax around. I carried her barbeque over to my front yard and fired it up. My heart was beating a little too fast with excitement. There were already a few more people here than there were last time.

I decided to bring the Mexican out to grill. I had cut him into pieces anyways and skinned him just in case anyone might notice it was familiar looking flesh. There was about 50 pounds of fresh slightly brown meat ready to go sliced into steaks like slabs. Ordinarily I would have saved the Mexican's meat for me as it was more like a steak when compared to the hookers. Theirs had a consistency like pork and wasn't quite as thick. For this though, it would be well worth it.

It was a Friday night so more people had work off the next day. It left more chance for nosy neighbors or people who may want to use my bathroom but I already planned to tell anyone like that that my bathroom was out of order. It was exciting to know I was going to get to see more people trying this meat I brought out tonight. My excitement was almost uncontrollable. I felt like a kid on Christmas who was getting to meet the real Santa.

I was officially introduced to my neighbor Steve this time. I had seen him before of course but we had never done much more than an acknowledging nod or wave. There may have been a time or two when we were both outside mowing and wound up talking for a few minutes about how it was quiet living around here and making weak promises to talk more later but that was about the extent of it.

It was good to finally talk to my neighbors. I was glad to calm any suspicions any of them might have had about me. My panic had begun to turn into something I could more easily ignore. With every bite someone else took of my food, a little part of the nervousness inside of me died. I felt like I could breathe again. I couldn't help but watch the mouths of each of the neighbors I was talking to as they licked the juices off their lips and fingers and swallowed the meat so happily trusting in the goodness of their fellow man. It was utterly amazing me how well this was going over. I found myself licking my own lips as I watched my neighbors each loving everything about this exotic grilled food. I found myself daydreaming about licking a couple peoples lips clean of the meats juices.

I put some of my favorite seasonings into it to give it kick and Yvonne at one point said, "Whew, this is some spicy stuff, did you use Mexican seasoning for this?" I had just taken a drink of my soda and it came shooting out of my nose before I could stop it. I was using every bit of will power I had not to burst out laughing. She looked at me curiously.

I quickly replied, with a little throat clear, "How did you guess that?"

She smiled and said, "I knew it!" and continued eating. If she only knew how badly I was dying inside, let alone why. I had to excuse myself to the restroom in my house just so I could let it out. I wondered if anyone heard me laughing inside. If so they never said anything about it. Before I left I had to go look in the mirror. I was surprised to see myself smiling; I hadn't smiled like this in so long. I think I was genuinely having a good time. I hadn't thought about killing a single neighbor either, besides Chris of course, but as expected, he never showed up.

Terry and Victoria didn't really say too much but they did eat plenty. I wondered how they would react if I let them know what exactly they just ate. They seemed nice though and the thought quickly left my mind. Victoria talked about a fundraiser she was putting together and let us all know we should definitely come to it. It was for another church member whose mother had fallen ill due to Cancer and they didn't think there was much time left for her. They kept the mother at her house instead of making her go to a hospital and the money was supposed to help cover the medical bills. Terry didn't say much at all. He seemed very much like the "Yes, dear" type of man.

The old couple didn't care to join us, Yvonne had already asked them. But she did bring them each a plate. The lonely wife with the missing husband joined us. Her name was Kira and she had been married for a couple of years to her husband Chris. He worked as a real estate negotiator in the United States as well as overseas. He was gone for at least five days a week and when he was home all he wanted to do was be on the phone in his private study, saying it was business and asking to be left alone so he could "relax." Kira tried doing everything for him from what Yvonne would tell me. Things like wearing lingerie and dancing for him. She would even try things like blowing him in the hallway or trying to surprise him with sneaky sex, but nothing she did seemed to work in her favor anymore.

I felt a sudden twinge of hate for this Chris guy. He had no idea what he had because Kira was beautiful. She had medium reddish blonde hair that flowed like a conditioner commercial. Gorgeous large green eyes and a very full set of luscious lips you would expect to see in a lipstick ad. She had a small nose almost the perfect size to be called button. Her body was beyond perfect. She did yoga and liked to work out in the mornings to keep in shape for Chris when he did come home. She didn't work and had always been a trust fund baby. She would never have to worry about money, especially now that her father had passed away and left her everything as his only child, the same as me.

She definitely didn't act as if she was gorgeous or well-off. Even when she ate the meat I brought to the barbeque, she only nibbled, apparently too self-conscious to let herself be seen eating like a normal person but it was cute to me. I felt a strange attraction to her, almost a possessive protective attraction. Maybe it was her innocence that drew me to her so much but I had other things to concentrate on so I settled for watching her eat for now.

There were a few other people that showed up from down the street as well such as one of Steve's cousins, a burly guy named Leroy who reminded me a bit of Larry the cable guy but was a lot taller and not nearly as funny.

Leroy had at least four of the steaks that I cooked. He asked me what kind of meat it was because to him it was familiar. I told him it was buffalo, to which he replied, "It couldn't be buffalo...buffalo's too tough." I said, "Not if you add my secret seasonings and beat the hell out of it."

Leroy chuckled. He had no idea about that I guess since he seemed to be satisfied that I was telling him the truth. He was also intoxicated and probably not the most aware he could be. He complimented me for making excellent meat better; slurping it down like it was going to cure his hangover tomorrow. He had more juices running down his face than anyone else here and I got goose bumps as he licked the juices from his fingers. I loved watching people eating human flesh. So many species of animals on the planet eat some species, some even eat their own and I was glad I could share this with so many of my own. It would have been much better if they all knew and willingly wanted to eat it. I would have to settle for this for now with cannibalism being so "taboo" but I was definitely going to have to make this a regular thing.

V.

It was a bright and sunny Saturday afternoon in the summer of 1994. I was 14 years old and at the very height of my adolescence. Summer break was almost over and I wanted to enjoy every last minute of it. I decided to walk to the store kill a craving and buy a soda and some kind of chocolaty snack. An ice cream bar definitely sounded like a good way to help beat this heat.

As I made my trek I was daydreaming about this girl I liked in school named Melissa Smith. I was also at the height of puberty and daydreamed about girls often, as young boys do. She was every boy's dream at my school but nobody even had the confidence to approach her or ask her for a date. She was in hindsight a lot like Kira, as far as being humble despite her awing beauty and attractive laid back attitude. She wasn't that stuck up hot girl you could imagine being head of the cheerleading squad and treating everyone like shit to amuse herself. Her smile could light up the entire school. She had huge dimples and gorgeous eyes and in the 8th grade she was already that girl who had surpassed even the hottest cheerleader in high school.

I was fantasizing about her asking me to kiss her as she stared at me with her big beautiful blue eyes. I knew it would never happen. She was way out of my league. As I walked it seemed the traffic was buzzing by me way too fast for a late afternoon. Everybody was in such a rush to get to wherever they were going and it seemed they were all late.

One of the cars, a late model sedan with dark tinted windows threw something out of their front passenger window as it drove by me. I didn't see it and it smacked me in the back of my head like a baseball bat knocking me forward.

I saw a bright light even in the sun and started to become disoriented. I tried to catch my balance but it happened so fast that I stumbled and tripped over my own feet, turning me backwards at the perfect angle to fall back into a jagged tree stump that was sticking out of the ground. There were a couple of broken off branches sticking out of the bottom of the trunk which stabbed into my upper left thigh right under my ass cheek.

Since I was still kind of out of it I couldn't coordinate my landing and the weight of my body pushed me even harder onto it. The force of my landing was enough to tear the skin apart resulting in a bloody mess near the crevasse of my butt cheeks making it look more than like I was bleeding from the rectum.

It happened to be a full bottle of soda that had smacked me in the back of the head. I looked down and saw the green bottle laying there all still like it had been there for a while. While I might laugh seeing a video of that happening to someone else, at this moment I was not amused. The overwhelming pain that burst into my focus was too much to bear and I started to cry. I was after all only 14 years old and not the best yet at keeping my emotions in check. I was also a little bit scared because I didn't know who the hell had done that to me. I didn't recognize the car and it was too dark to see inside in the short time I had before collision.

So I was sitting there bleeding from my ass and crying on the side of the street when all of a sudden the car that had thrown the bottle had turned around and started driving back towards me. It was none other than Lucas, the most hated bully in my school. Somehow I wasn't surprised when I saw him leaning out of the window grinning menacingly at me. He was a skinny but strong red headed freckle faced asshole. He didn't care about getting into trouble as anything they ever did to him stopped nothing.

It was like the school wanted to protect him as if he were the fragile one and not the instigator every time. He liked to pick on many kids, at the very least myself every chance he got. His demeanor was like that of a long time prison inmate who had only gotten worse from learning the ways of intimidation and abuse to get what they wanted. If they kept coddling his bad behavior, he was just a kid right now, where was this going to end later on when he was even more capable?

The air had to be drying out his disgustingly dirty brace filled mouth as he began laughing at me with his head hanging out the window. "Awe, poor baby gonna cry over his first period?" He seemed to be thoroughly enjoying himself, which for once, made me mad.

The last thing I heard before I started to see red was his laughter, which somehow had become the most annoying sound in the world to me. Something had snapped inside of my head and I felt the blood start rushing into my face. All at once it became too much, I don't know if it was shock, or he had knocked something loose in my brain. But I started running after the car he was in, which surprised him. I felt like my eyeballs were bulging and filling with blood. I had never done anything but take it from him any time he came at me. I had taken all of his shit, all of his torturous abuse never doing anything about it but clamming up inside. This had to be the last straw, this time he had gone too far.

I hauled ass, running after them, I ran faster than I had ever run before, despite my fucked up ripped open ass cheek. I felt like I could almost jump up into the wind and fly towards them I was running so fast and I was pissed.

I could hear his buddy the driver saying, "Oh shit here she comes."

What an asshole, I thought to myself, but I got his "she" right in the middle of my balled up fist. I wanted nothing more than to rip his head off and kick him right in the face over and over again, both of them. I was so furious. His buddy put the gas to the floor and there was no way I was going to catch up after that. I watched as the car pulled away, a lasting smile on the face of my assailant that I would never forget.

I don't remember the walk home; I only remember that I couldn't think of anything else. His friend who had been the shit talker this time was a sophomore but I wasn't afraid of him. I was surprising myself but it seemed that I wasn't softening up about this. The fact that they had driven off told me a lot about their mentality. If I was going to make some sort of stand, I would have to have the courage to stand up to them through whatever comes my way.

I would never back down again, the time for being afraid passed when I was attacked in the middle of a daydream and I wasn't even at school. Later that night as I sat there in the tub soaking my torn skin in the bath trying to feel a bit more normal after my embarrassing exhibition, I started to feel that old familiar rage. All the times he had picked on me started running through my mind.

There were a couple of times he had grabbed me by the shirt dragging me into the bathroom without me able to fight back or too scared to and proceeded to pull my head by the hair forcing me to stick my face in the toilet. He would then put his knee in my back and then put all his weight he could on me, forcing my face into the water making sure I stayed there for a few seconds extra before I could get up. I could feel other hands and I knew a couple of his buddies were pushing me down with them. The worst part was that he never gave me a normal swirly. It was always in the toilet he and his friends had made sure to piss in that he would stick my face in.

There was another time he embarrassed me in front of a few of the hottest girls in the school. He came up behind me while I was walking by them and de-pants me so my junk was completely exposed for all to see. They would always laugh and look at each other as if to say look at that loser.

Other times, he would run up behind me in the hallways and kick at just the right moment to clip the foot stepping forward making me trip over myself falling forward too fast for a normal stumble. No, that could never be enough for him. Along with a nice trip he would also push me it seemed with all his might, so that my weight and his push would slam my face into the locker so hard it would damn near bend it open leaving me with a bloody face and a near broken nose. He would tell me then that if I said anything he was going to break my arm.

No, he has to learn some kind of lesson. I'm done being afraid of him. I felt more of the rage boil as I thought of how absolutely great of a feeling it would be to stuff his head into a toilet full of wet nasty diarrhea. I was able to laugh at least while thinking of devious ways to get him back. I was minding my own business trying to enjoy my summer and he pulls that shit on me? Then to have him talk about me having a period! I'm sick of his ass. I wanted to beat him with a rock until he quits moving.

Nobody stopped to help me either or even said anything. I know a few people saw it because I could see them slow down to gawk before continuing on their way. I wish I could just beat all of them too. If shit continued on like this I might as well just hang a sign on my neck saying, "I'm everybody's little bitch." I made up my mind right then and there. I was going to be worse than he could ever be. I would make him terrified of me.

Terrified.

VI.

The next day as I walked into school, I was careful not to rub the stab wound on my ass as I walked. It probably needed a couple of stitches but I had stitch taped it together in the mirror the best I could and with enough pressure, it eventually closed up on its own. It was still sensitive though, even my backpack rubbing on it two weeks later killed me. I walked to my locker about the same speed as an old man with a hip injury would have, taking small, calculated steps. As I was putting my stuff into my locker and getting what I needed for my first class, I saw Lucas out of the corner of my eye looking at me.

I pretended not to notice him just then because I knew that the mere sight of me seeing him would bring him my way. I was a bit nervous today, not feeling quite as up to this as I was last night. That quickly changed for me though, he started walking towards me smiling that same cocky smile he always had. That was all the motivation I needed to bring back the hate and anger I felt for him last night. It came back to my foremost thoughts like a wave.

Before school, I had grabbed a heavy little paperweight from my mom's kitchen drawer. It wasn't a seriously threatening thing, but I'm sure it would do some damage. It was just a little metal eagle with a solid heavy bottom and sturdy pointed wings as if he were trying to take off flying. However it was at least a full pound of weight and the wings were such that I could hold it with them and it fit into my hand just right with the metal solid end sticking out in front of my fists. I knew that it would be enough since I tested how damaging it could be on my closet door. I could hit it and my hand didn't even get hurt but the wood was now splintered in a couple of spots.

As he walked towards me I slowly and with stealth put my hand in my pocket and slid it into my hand. "What's up daddy's little girl?" he asked with a sneer. He reached out to grab my shoulder with his left hand, as if he was going to intimidate me today. In one quick move I pulled out the paperweight, bent down and slammed it hard sideways into his thigh giving him the worst Charlie horse he had probably ever had.

He bent down to instinctively grab his throbbing leg. I took that opportunity to bring it down sideways on the side of his head. I didn't want to hit him too hard, just enough to stun him and hopefully bruise the inside of his head. While he was stunned, I ran behind him as fast as I could and I started bringing my knee forward into his tailbone again and again as hard as I could holding his shoulders to pull him back even more into each solid hit.

After a few blows he was no longer standing anymore. He fell through my grasp and began rolling around on the floor. It was funny how fast he fell and honestly surprised me, but I wasn't done with him yet.

His friends were standing there in shock, but as puzzled as they looked they still tried to jump in and grab me. I bit the first kids hand hard enough to draw blood and hit him in the head with the little weight. Not too hard, but it knocked him out. I looked at his other buddy and asked, "You want some too?" To which he turned tail and ran, I'm sure to go tell the principal.

The asshole kid, Lucas, was still lying there holding his tailbone. "I'm going to kick your ass!" he looked like he was about to cry.

I couldn't help but laugh at him looking so pathetic. I replied, "Yeah somehow I think you're done kicking ass today." I then slammed the weight into his shoulder a couple of times... hard. I swore I could feel the bone nearly give in with the first hit and then I smacked the other shoulder a couple of times before climbing over the top of him. I started slapping him front and backhand in the face. For every time he had ever given me the urge to hide. For every time he scared me or made me feel like less than him.

His nose started bleeding so I stopped slapping him. I didn't want to get his blood all over me. He started to get some sense back and he started crying. He hadn't expected this, and he was afraid of me at the moment. I smacked him again in the head; I wanted him to just relax for a moment. He was knocked out long enough for me to undo his pants and pull them down just below his ass cheeks. I looked at his unbroken skin and before I could help myself, I stabbed him with one of the wings in the left cheek. He started bleeding a steady little flow similar to mine that day and I pulled his pants back up so he could look like he was bleeding from the ass.

He was unable to do much but scream for help and cry as he started to come to. He tried to push himself up but his shoulders still hurt and he fell back to the floor. I got down to his level and laughed in his face. I put the wing up to his face right in front of his eye and lowered my head towards his speaking in a menacing voice. "Don't cry, it's just a period." I stood up and put my paperweight back in my pocket and waited for the principal, delightedly watching him as he cried and cowered, shaking on the floor.

After a couple of minutes I could hear the footsteps of the principal and when he approached I could see Lucas's little buddy right behind him. The principal looked at me in awe, as if he had never seen anything like this before. Here he stood over a kid lying on the ground who was a known bully with bloody pants looking like he did indeed, have a bloody period. Standing next to him was a nerdy, but fed up, calm kid who had taken control and punished him.

After he figured out what was going on I could tell the principal was trying to stifle laughter. He seemed just like the guy who himself used to get picked on and I'm sure on some level he was happy to see this but he couldn't just let it go. He knew he had to say something. The principal looked at me, standing there calmly and asked what happened. I said, "I'm tired of being bullied, so I took matters into my own hands to stop him. I could see the principal wasn't quite disappointed so much as amused by it. Still somehow keeping his reserve, he let us know that we were both going to have to be suspended for fighting. There was a zero tolerance policy on violence in the school and in the future, we should talk things out rather than become physical. I also could have sworn he winked at me before turning around to lead the way to the office for the both of us.

So a little slap on the wrist is all I had gotten for that! I hadn't done too much damage. He had some bumps and cuts but mostly I just embarrassed him by making him get a couple of stitches. Surprisingly, his father never wanted to press charges for the damage I'd done. I suspect he wasn't very happy about it though since Lucas came back to school with more bruises and sore muscles than I had given him. I'm sure it was from his father teaching him to be a real man. I was happy with that because after all, that was what I was going for in the first place.

From then on it was like that. I would see him in the halls and if I didn't like how he looked at me I would approach him and attack him. He tried a couple of times to stand up to me but I would just hammer the shit out of him with my fists as hard as I could. I made sure to hit him in the throat with a nice open handed chop to get his eyes watering and then I would follow up with some full force punches anywhere I could land them. I would swing over and over until I felt like stopping or he ran away. More and more of my punches started connecting the more often I did it so it was also good practice. The other kids thought I was bat-shit crazy, but nobody liked him anyways so they never said a thing to the principal.

I was becoming less and less afraid the more I messed him up and everyone was becoming scared of me. I found that the more relentless I was, the scarier I became to them. Soon enough, it must have been about a good month; Lucas didn't so much as even look my way anymore. If he did, he knew I would run up and get crazy, lumping him up with fresh knots and bruises as much as I could. He didn't dare tell the principal, his dad would have beaten him even more. He just started covering his face most of the time and letting me pound on him until I was done. I'm sure he had gotten a lot of practice at home with that. A few times of that and he did the best he could to avoid me.

I loved the feeling of power I got from terrorizing the school bully and having him be afraid of me! It was one of the best feelings I could ever have after being the kid that was once bullied. I still wasn't satisfied. I could remember another time when he would take my lunch and try to stuff it in my face, putting his nasty cock grabbing hands on my food, ruining it for me. I was beginning to get some dark thoughts running through my head.

He grabbed the pudding another kid had brought for lunch one time and smeared it all over the poor kids head and then spit into his juice and made him drink it. To me enough was enough. Why had nobody ever done anything to him? He got away with too much already, it had to stop. He was rotten to the core and I think a huge part of that rubbed off on me. He was definitely going to have to pay for past crimes. I had a flash in my mind that stopped me in my tracks of slicing off one of his ass cheeks making him half assed. Then I got to thinking, I couldn't leave him like that. I mean, I had never been in trouble with the law or anything, but I'm sure for a couple cut off asscheeks, I would probably be locked away in a mental institution for a while. No, I think I would somehow have to make him disappear. Like Jimmy Hoffa. I rolled my eyes and kind of laughed at the idea. Imagine me, at 14, becoming my own mafia-style body disposal man. The only difference being I wouldn't be disposing for the mafia but for myself, for my own ass to be covered. All of a sudden I was standing there with my mouth open at the idea that I was actually sitting here thinking of shit like this. I was kind of serious too.

I decided to let the fantasy go on. I had actually heard stories of a couple bodies being supposedly dumped down at this old swamp through the woods and it actually wasn't very far from my house. Letting the fantasy take me I thought, *How the hell would I be able to carry a body down the probably two mile path to the swamp?* First of all, I didn't believe I was that strong and second; me carrying a body would obviously raise some questions if anyone happened to see me.

What if I had to run, what then? You know, as odd as it seems answers seemed to come automatically to me about how I could do these things and get away with it. The answers I was getting kind of scared me at first. The first thing that came to mind was to cut the body up into pieces. While I wasn't sure I could actually stomach that, the idea oddly enough did appeal to me.

I remembered going hunting with my uncle when I was about 8 or 9 and when he shot this deer right through the head I wasn't sure how to feel. I do remember thinking that it didn't even know it was about to be shot and didn't have a chance in hell of survival. I thought how unfair that was. When the gutting commenced, I remembered the putrid foul stench vividly from the fresh guts when my uncle took them out of its body. I remembered gagging at the stench.

I started gagging now, just remembering the smell. It looked cool as the guts slid off each other until they were in a slimy pile of stench you didn't really ever want to have to smell. You didn't really notice the smell though when you're watching the guts falling out. I didn't think I had that in me. I think if the smell of deer guts was enough to get me gagging; I wasn't going to be able to carry a dead body anyways, so I laughed the fantasy away.

VII.

I found myself standing in the middle of a very dark and creepy forest. There was complete darkness in the trees that surrounded me on all sides. There was nearly zero visibility and I couldn't see more than the shadows of the trees no matter how badly I wanted to. I wasn't quite sure what was going on. I knew it was supposed to be cold but I didn't feel uncomfortable at all, just creeped out by the impossible blackness of this place. Something about it just seemed… empty.

At the same time it was like there was a strong presence all around me. A long dark path was ahead of me that I could faintly make out after I had that thought. A bright light that hadn't been there a moment ago appeared in the distance. The light looked to be moving away slowly. I wasn't sure exactly where I was which didn't really bother me but I didn't want to get stuck again in the dark, so I hurried towards it. I noticed a foul smell all around me. It was akin to rotting food that had been left in a warm refrigerator. It was like something that had spoiled well beyond its expiration date.

The light was fading fast but I kept heading towards it as fast as I could manage. The smell was getting stronger now and gaining a copper-like edge to it. The smell was similar to your hands after handling hundreds of old pennies. It also had a hint of old wet metal to it somehow.

I looked up to my right as I felt something brush my shoulder but I couldn't make out what it was even though there was a faraway light softly illuminating the path. I found out that it was warm and wet though when I reached my hand up to make sure it wasn't just a tree branch poking me.

I wanted to see what the hell could be warm, slimy and wet in a tree although the combination sounded like something I probably didn't want the answer to. It was incredibly dark out and it had rained which had made the ground soggy because my shoes were sucking into the ground as they might in a muddy yard. I wished that I could see.

All of a sudden a light illuminated the area as if a bright spotlight were shined down on me. It seemed to be pointing everywhere I wanted to see now which I found odd. Infact, it was only shining in the places I wanted to look. I couldn't see everything but it showed me like a flashlight what was there behind the darkness. I could now see in the light that seemed to come from nowhere what was hanging on the trees and had been brushing my shoulder.

It was a series of large and small intestines and various other slimy body parts dripping wet with blood, which seemed to be covering everything. It was on the trees and the ground... everywhere. It was like I was inside of a giant body only instead of cells swimming down a river of blood, there were body parts. I panicked and started running away, though I had no idea where I was going.

The light seemed to follow me wherever I would go, which was nice because I could see where I was going. It was also demoralizing, since all I could see was blood on the ground and organs and other body parts in all of the trees. As I ran, I tripped over a thigh that was lying on the ground and fell headfirst into what I mistook at first as a shallow pool of blood on the ground. I realized right away it was nothing of the sort.

I had fallen into what had become a deep little blood swamp and my entire body was able to go under the bloody surface. When I came up I was covered in blood just as much as any of these body parts and organs in this forest. I reached out to see if I could feel the edge of what I thought was a little puddle but I couldn't find an edge. It was as if it were moving around just to avoid my hands. Or I had teleported into an ocean of thick mucus like blood. The worst part was that now I couldn't see and had nothing even semi-clean to try and wipe some of this blood out of my eyes.

I could feel something floating next to me. I couldn't tell what it was at first but when I felt with my hand as I tried desperately to keep afloat I felt what could only be a human torso missing the rest of its limbs. To my horror I could also now feel on my suddenly bare feet what could only be a human head in this nightmare from the deepest pits of hell. I scrambled around in this mess of meat and felt more dismembered pieces surrounding my terrified self. There must have been at least four bodies in this blood puddle alone.

I wanted to feel the edge so bad and suddenly I could feel it again. I tried scrambling to get out every way that I could but it was soon evident that it was no use. Every movement that I made no matter how careful even or how small seemed to stir up the bodies around me which made them move into just the wrong spot like right in front of my chest just as I was about to jump up. I was feeling weaker by the minute.

A head had floated up from the bottom and was bobbing in a weird bloody ripple of pressure that came from the bottom just to the right of me. It was barely attached to its body by a bit of neck flesh and when I looked down seemed to roll so I could see the face. Another burst of pressure from underneath the bodies that were more on the bottom came up and lifted the head up and over as if it was pushing it towards me. I could feel its moustache and nose rub on me as it slimed the entire side of my face.

I started screaming and reached out to push the body away. It was heavier than I had figured and I lost my balance, going back and losing my footing as a body I was stepping on slipped out from under me. I went under enough that my head was under the blood again which this time since I went under mid scream, filled up my mouth.

After I got my footing back I moved the body parts underneath the blood with my foot until I managed to stack together a couple of the torsos down there so I could get a better step up and get the hell out of here. I still had this guys nearly decapitated body in front of me so I used the torsos to get more push and with all my might lifted up the body again in front of me. It was very slippery and seemed almost like it was being pushed from behind it onto me.

The weight of it above me made it hard to get a good balance as my hands kept slipping off of it and my feet were barely able to stay where they were. I was losing this battle and the weight of the body on top of me slowly sunk me under the surface. I could feel the hair of one of the heads rubbing against my face as I used my arms and legs to push the body off of me and get back above the surface.

When I got back to the surface I started to vomit, I couldn't help it. I couldn't breathe and almost choked on the blood that now coated my entire respiratory system. I was beginning to shake uncontrollably. I was scared now, more scared than I had ever been. I couldn't get out of here and this is nowhere I wanted to die. I became a little angry though as my shivering had made the puddle move again pushing the body back up and in front of me once more.

I put my hands closer together and pushed trying to shove the body backwards from me. I succeeded finally and the body went back away from me… but the head didn't. The slimy bloody head came forward, hitting my own forehead with his. Its bloated lips attempting to smear a jelly like goo on my lips and some of the blood from its mouth poured into mine stopping my ability to scream or breathe. I once more started choking on the blood that felt like it was trying to coagulate in my throat. I wished for there to be an end to this horror.

From out of nowhere a humongous tree branch came to life swooping down and picking me out of the bloody nightmarish puddle by my midsection. The sudden strong motion of my body jerking against the branch as it pulled me up worked like the Heimlich maneuver. It was enough to help force the chunky mess up and I projection vomited the blood in my throat that I had begun to unwillingly swallow out. I gasped for as much rotten gaseous air as I could get. The tree had grabbed me around the chest and under my arms; I felt like a ragdoll in the hands of a giant.

I was being held a good 12 feet in the air by a fucking tree. I had a sudden flash that this was a dream. I breathed a sigh of relief. This must be the part where I wake up and realize I am having a nightmare. I could still taste the blood though and smell the gaseous air and feel the tree's strength. If it wanted to I felt it could have easily squeezed me in half. I tried to wriggle my body just to see if there was any chance of escaping, to no avail.

The tree drew me closer to it, directly in front of itself which I could see thanks to the spotlight that was still following me now acting more like moonlight while shining on the gigantic deep black hole a foot in front of me. The light was just enough to see there was a hole there but for some reason I couldn't see inside of it no matter how hard I tried squinting my eyes. I felt like this giant tree was staring at me, as if this hole was a supernatural eye that could see right through me. I had the feeling that this tree was ancient. I could feel an infinite wisdom just being in the present of this monolith. This was definitely the presence I had felt earlier.

A loud booming voice came out of the tree that seemed to penetrate my very head like a deep, powerful bass that makes you feel like your heart might stop. I was still shaking. "YOU ARE NOT A VICTIM! THE BLOOD MAKES IT REAL!" I said nothing, but even with all the blood on my face the tree seemed to know how I felt because I was completely confused what he meant.

It took my body and tightened its grip a bit and shoved me into the 6 foot in diameter hole in its face. It felt like I was placed into something like a blanket of air. Gravity was nonexistent here and it was once again completely dark. I could feel that I was floating but there was no tension trying to drag me down, or up or any way at all. I tried looking out of the hole I was just put into and I couldn't see anything. Not even an inch outside of the hole! I couldn't even see the hole anymore that was how dark it had gotten.

A faint light started to glow from the nothingness in front of me and it began growing brighter as I watched it. Soon it started to more resemble something like a television screen that was becoming clearer and brighter, until it seemed as if I could reach right into the incredibly clear picture and touch what I was looking at.

I could see a person more clearly as the picture focused and I realized before long that I was looking at myself, or at least someone who resembled a possible future version of me. I was somewhere in my early 20's if I was to guess and much more muscular than I am now. I tried again to look around but I still couldn't see anything. Not even with light was there even a hint of a border in this impossible blackness. The only thing that was visible was the scene unfolding in front of me. It was as if I were in the total blackness of space itself except for the portal like television I was watching my future self on.

I looked back at the vision unfolding before me, where I appeared completely obsessed with my task at hand. That disturbed me since from what I could see looked to be cutting up a human male. He was probably around 30 years old and had a look of shock on his face as if he'd just been walked in on while masturbating. The older me had been sweating, but I'll be damned if he seemed anything but at ease with what he was doing. I kept watching as he expertly sawed between joints and dismembered this body like he had done it a million times before. I was absolutely aghast with what I was witnessing.

What really came as a surprise to me though was what he did next. He began cutting the meat off of the bones and putting them into gallon sized sealable baggies and putting them in the freezer. I was confused why my future self would do that but I kept watching. I noticed a plate was there in front of my older self. I couldn't even begin to imagine it was what I thought it was after seeing the bagging of body parts. It looked like a pork chop, only with no bone and a bit thicker from what I could see. I watched as the older me cut off a piece, put it into his mouth, chewed it up and swallowed it.

I figured the meat was already cooked from the dark color of it but when the future me took that first bite, he had blood oozing from his mouth between his teeth and starting to drip down his chin. I blinked and looked away for a second feeling a bit nauseous and when I looked back at him I saw no blood, only a drip from what looked to be some very juicy meat. My stomach growled at that, catching me by surprise.

Suddenly, the light grew dim on the screen until it was once again dark. The smell in the tree was faint but similar to mushrooms now. The light brightened up in another spot to my right as another vision began to unfold. I was a bit older than before by maybe 5 years, eating what looked like a chicken noodle soup and reading a newspaper.

Just like the light earlier that would shine where I was trying to look; the viewpoints in this TV seemed to go everywhere I wanted to see as well. I could make it zoom in or out, circle the view around to get just the vantage points I wanted. It was like there was a disembodied cameraman filming from all the most convenient angles I could possibly want to see.

I settled on checking out what he was eating at the moment, just out of curiosity. I could see noodles and meat, peas and various veggies. I sighed with relief thinking it was indeed chicken noodle soup. Then, when my older self moved his spoon, I could see from my vantage point what was, unmistakably; a human eyeball. It looked small and kind of like a squished grape, but I had no doubt in my mind that it was an eyeball from the skull of Homo erectus. It was a blue eye I'm sure at one point but the color had since faded to an empty dark gray.

My older self put the spoon in the bowl again, and then to his lips, drank the juice and then ate the eye without even batting one of his own. It looked like I was really at peace with eating people. I couldn't read my older selves mind in the future, but I could see a smile forming on his face. I looked to see what he was reading that was bringing a smile to my older lips. It was a story about a missing man who had been dismembered. His hands and testicles were sent to his father and mother with a note saying:

"These hands you brought into this world have hurt children.

Do the right thing. Never have another!"

Your sons killer.

Future me finished his bowl, licked his lips and put the bowl in the sink and rinsed it off. Future me burped loudly, seemingly satisfied with his meal. I followed behind him to see what my older self was seeing as he went to the freezer and opened it. There on the shelf next to a half empty jug of milk, sat a human head… and his eyes were missing.

I vomited in the tree and woke up sitting in my bed, sweating. I could almost smell actual vomit. I checked to see if I had thrown up in my bed in my sleep. I saw none and the smell soon faded. My stomach was growling, I remembered that I hadn't eaten any dinner last night before I fell asleep. That was one crazy ass dream! I couldn't get the thought out of my head how good that meal seemed to be, by the look on my future face. I tried not to think about the eyes though because that was instant nausea.

I began having that same dream repeatedly almost every night after that. It had been a few months now and I had grown used to having it anymore. I had even started looking around a bit more in my dream. I still didn't recognize the forest that the tree was in, or the faces of the people in the bloody puddle that I couldn't seem to avoid no matter how much I paid attention. It was to the point where I could walk to the area where the light starts to lead the way without guidance. No matter how much I tried to deviate though I would always wind up in the bloody puddle.

I just couldn't seem to avoid gagging on blood and the coppery aftertaste as I almost choked to death. Yet every time, I would be saved by the tree which would promptly put me inside of its body where I would watch myself in the future dismember and cannibalize dead humans in many various scenarios. So far, while I was in it, I hadn't noticed that I was actually dreaming other than expecting to wake up from a nightmare towards the end. It's so realistic to me while I'm in it that I can't help but feel it's real. At least I didn't puke myself awake anymore.

VIII.

It had been almost half of the school year now since I decided enough was enough with Lucas and finally stood up to him and the other bullies he hung out with. My schoolwork and grades had improved exponentially. I was able to concentrate more on getting things done rather than thinking about what was the least dangerous way to walk to my next class. I didn't worry about that anymore. I knew him and his friends were all just a bunch of talk once they realized I was going to stand up for myself. Lucas was the worst of them all with picking on weak kids, but I had him self-conscious now. I laid off of running up to fight him when I would see him in the halls now but he knew better than to test me. It was confusing anymore as to who was the actual bully between the two of us when I was now the one giving unprovoked beatings.

I had been having the bloody forest dream so much lately, pretty much every single night. Every time I fell asleep it seemed it was surrounding me, there was nothing that I could do to stop it. I felt like I was trapped in some kind of Freddy movie and couldn't fall asleep or the puddle of blood would choke me to death. One day in school, I was in study hall with nothing to do, I had done all of my homework in my other classes while the teacher yapped on with their various politics and opinions. Whatever I needed was in the books they told us to open so I would read them and do my lessons while they talked. Sometimes the teachers would be so boring that I would do the next three or more days of lessons just to get them done with for the week. This day I decided to lay my head down on my desk. Nobody was talking or they were sleeping or focused on their studies themselves. There was a low hum from the lights in the room that began lulling me to sleep before I even realized it was happening.

I found myself in the dark of the forest and I began to have the nightmare once again. I was slipping in blood and had a couple throatfuls of it already. Luckily this time, before too much near drowning could happen I felt a smack on my back from the kid next to me that woke me up with a yell. The whole class was looking at me. Some of them looked concerned while others looked like they wanted to laugh. The kid sitting next to me asked if I was hung over or something because I kept gagging in my sleep. He thought I was going to puke. I was drenched in sweat, embarrassed and worried that I had this dream in the daytime. I ran out of the class without a word, hearing scattered laughter behind me and went to the bathroom so I could splash some cold water on my face. I looked myself in the eyes; I was starting to feel like I was going crazy.

Sometimes in the dreams I would find myself wondering what it would taste like as I watched my older self devour the human meats in so many different ways. I was beginning to feel like it wasn't such a big deal seeing so much post death cannibalism having dealt with choking and almost drowning in blood every night for months now. I wondered if I was ever going to get a dreamless night again, or at least a dream that didn't involve blood and cannibalism.

For one of my year end school assignments, I got to write a paper on who was my all-time hero. It didn't have to be my actual hero; the teacher just wanted me to write a story that explained why the person I picked could be a hero to someone. I was excited to write this story, anything to distract me from sleeping at night. For my class assignment, I found a story about a man who was a German innkeeper from Silesia. He loved to eat what he liked to call 'The Long Pig.' His basis for the name was that he said human meat was similar to pig meat. I actually thought about this before watching my dream self chewing on it while the sausage like juices dripped down his chin.

Both pigs and humans actually have similar skin. I have heard about people that liked to do tattoos on pigs since they had the most similar skin to a human. I also heard that pig's organs had successfully been experimented with inside of a human body, by removing the cells in them from the pig, the organ would turn white. The cells of the human would then be pumped through the organ and when implanted, the body would accept the organ as its own. That alone told me that we indeed had similar bodies and probably did indeed taste the same.

Of course, this German was in real life a cannibal, so I was absolutely interested in what he had to say about it. As the story goes, over the course of his murderous career in inn keeping he killed more than thirty of his lodgers and kept their pickled remains in the basement of his inn. I wondered what pickled remains tasted like. Would the vinegar make the meat taste sour, like some kind of a meat pickle? When he was arrested in 1924, he told the police that for the past three years he had eaten nothing but human flesh. I remembered feeling a bit of jealousy that he had gotten to eat that much human meat. I wondered what changed in me that I should feel like that but I was jealous nonetheless.

Were my dreams really starting to affect me? I thought to myself as I was walking in the halls. I heard a stifled yell for help and I walked up the hallway and turned the corner listening for the sound I heard before. It came even fainter than before and I heard from the bathroom a sound I knew all too well. There was someone in there getting a swirly. My first thought of course was that it was Lucas, which made me forget what had just happened in class. My blood was about to start boiling I was so hot when I ran into the bathroom.

I was pleasantly surprised when I saw the asshole and two of his friends holding a nerdy kid's head inside a surprisingly clean toilet. They must not have put too much nasty shit in there this time because his head looked like there had only been clean water in there when they started.

That actually pissed me off a little bit more since they had always made mine nasty before. Lucas looked over and when he saw me walk in he instantly let go of the kid as a worried look spread across his face. I could see him looking at my waist, probably looking for a bulge that might be hiding a paperweight again. There was none, but it didn't stop me from rushing his first buddy and shoving his head backwards into the stall with all the force I had. He cracked his head hard and fell to the floor unconscious. I stared at Lucas and his other buddy who had also now let go of the little guy they had been picking on.

"You just don't learn, do you?!" I said to Lucas, who was visibly shaken.

"Whatever man, its clean water in there, anyways, I haven't even looked your way or talked to you lately, so just leave me alone alright? I've gotta go I'm going to be late for class." He turned around and walked out quickly as he could with both his buddies. They had both helped the one I knocked out who woke up after about 30 seconds. They slinked out with him holding his head. I stood there shaking with rage inside and my plans were shifting to a darker path as I stood there looking at this poor little blond haired coke bottle glasses nerd. He was crying and embarrassed at what had just happened to him. "Thanks", he mustered with the might of a mouse as he wiped some snot and tears from his face with his arm at the wrist, and then picked up his books.

"No problem." I held the door open for him as he ran out, leaving a trail of toilet water behind him. I wasn't going to be around to help him all the time. Things were going to have to get a bit more drastic than my beating Lucas' ass I was afraid. He was going to have to go away…
permanently.

IX.

It was summer vacation now and I had seriously begun to plot the murder of Lucas. I got myself on a serious workout regimen once I first began to fight back. I figured it would be worse to get beaten after trying to fight back than to just force myself to build a bit of muscle on my body. It took serious dedication, how much I had no idea when I started. I had grown quite a bit since last summer when they pushed me to the limit. It seemed I was actually becoming a bit intimidating. I just wanted to be scarier to them every day.

I was almost sixteen now and the fact that he no longer picked on anybody or looked my direction had no effect on my decision. He pushed it too far too soon and now I just had the compulsion to hate him forever and kill him still. Maybe it was the recurring nightmare that I had been having, I felt compelled now to see this through. In my awakened and desensitized new way of thinking, this was becoming an obsession rather than something that simply happened in a dream. I had even started to think about it as less of a nightmare and more of a dream. I wasn't sure how to feel about that but then again my emotions had become less important the more I was subjected to this repeating dark vision.

I began to follow him home when he left school. I had no idea before I did that but he lived almost right behind me if

I were to cut through the woods behind my property. It was still about a half a mile walk but my plan became that much easier now that it was so close to where I lived. Besides, I had nothing but time on my hands, I was going to learn everything about his home and life that I could.

I learned when his mother left for work, and what time she would get home, which was the same pretty much every night, about 9 o'clock. She always looked happy when she left in the afternoons but when she got home she would sit in the car for fifteen minutes or so before finally getting out to go inside. I was curious what she was doing so trying not to be obvious, I would stand back and watch her from the shadows the best I could. She was just talking to the face staring back at her in the rearview mirror as if she had to talk herself in to going back to the life she had waiting for her inside. Sometimes she just had to gather herself up after crying on the drive home. I was immediately attracted to her.

Lucas' father stayed at home everyday drinking and chain-smoking. Occasionally he would come outside to check the mail. He was probably waiting for some government check for sitting on his ass all day pretending to be disabled. It seemed to work for him, he sat at home all day collecting money watching tv and she went out working as a waitress, paying all the bills because what he had he spent on escape in a bottle. Which, in itself meant that someone was always going to be home so any plans of doing this at his house were out of the question. The simplest way to get caught is by having witnesses in the first place. I remained vigilant and followed him around anyways. Everything I had read, or been shown about killing showed that a good murderer needed to know their victims patterns. If nothing else, maybe it would teach me why he was such an asshole.

I watched him night after night from the darkness of the trees at the edge of their yard where nobody could see me. One night, as he went inside, instead of going out and watching from the edge of the tree line, I decided to walk around to the left side behind the house and really see what was going on inside. There were three windows and a backdoor on the back side of the house. There was a window on the left which I have gathered by watching was Lucas' bedroom. It had the curtains opened but the light was off at the moment making it pitch black. Then there was a window which looked to be the kitchen, it was also dark but I could see the light from the living room in the front of the house through it. Then there was another bedroom window to the right side that I could see through since the curtains were drawn back and the light was on.

I suspect they didn't expect anyone to be inside the yard looking in so they didn't worry about the curtains being open. If you were to look out their windows you would see the tree line and then just dark forest. I'm sure they didn't think that there was some psycho peeping into their rooms from this side of the house. The window was open about six inches and I could hear the voice of his mother asking,

"Do you know where my blow-dryer is?" She was standing in front of the mirror in the master bathroom, straight to the back of the room, where I was standing looking through the window. I could see her pretty well from where I was.

"What do I look like, keeper of all useless SHIT women need?" The drunken reply I could only assume was Lucas father. I could picture him sitting in his lazy boy drinking a cheap beer barely acknowledging anything but the television. He continued on, "You need to keep an eye on your own shit, how am I gonna know where your shit is if I'm all the way in here trying to enjoy myself and I gotta worry about keeping track of your shit." I could see her roll her eyes as he carried on. Obviously he had no idea. I could actually see it lying on the bed; she must have just forgotten she put it there.

She came out of the bathroom and into the bedroom dressed in a semi see-through light blue nighty with a towel wrapped around her head. She must have just gotten out of the shower. I felt a sudden regret that I missed seeing it. I could see about half of both her breasts which were surprisingly ample and still very nice for her age. It was enough to cause a hard-on to start growing. Her chest looked so soft and I'll bet she would be nice and warm against me.

I could feel my heart starting to pound now as she went to the mirror in the bathroom again and grabbed a bottle of lotion. She squirted some onto her hands and began softly rubbing it on her chest and neck. I kept watching as she slowly moved her hands down to her stomach and then her legs. I could tell she was thinking about something other than moisturization by the way she was rubbing it in so slowly. Her feeling turned on was enough for me to start touching myself without noticing I was even doing it. I thought for a second and decided what the hell. She couldn't see me out here it was too dark, and I could be fast, I knew from experience.

I let my hand guide itself inside of my pants where it pulled my dick out and started stroking it to her. I began slowly at first, trying to build it up and enjoy getting lost in the fantasy, then my stroking got a bit faster until I was pounding it in my hand. As I looked at her in the mirror I realized that she was actually very hot. Her face was one of a kind beautiful; she had full kissable lips and model high cheekbones.

Her face could very well have been sculpted by Aphrodite herself, I was amazed she was with this drunken mess of a husband she had. She had nice round perky tits and a very well-shaped athletic looking midsection. A great tight round ass and delectable come fuck me eyes with gorgeous long lashes. I had seen her before, but never in all of her naked glory. I had also never seen her without clothing on.

I could see her white panties turning a more fleshy color near her crotch as she started warming up. I could tell she was clean shaven too, I could see the folds where her tight little lips hugged her panties. As I kept stroking, I started thinking about how wet she could be for me, especially with no hair there, soaking up her sweet nectars. Then my thoughts turned to how it would feel to fuck her while she cried over her dead son. That last thought almost stopped me from stroking but it was too late. I started to cum and it wouldn't stop.

I don't think that even in all my times masturbating as a horny teenager, it had ever been this good or I had cum so hard. I felt like It would never stop as I stood there stroking every last drop onto the ground beneath her window. I hoped nobody looked out while I was in the midst of it because I had stopped paying any attention. I returned there to get my rocks off a few more times over the next few weeks. I stopped after one time that I peeped in on her and she was fucking the drunk. The thought of her fucking that drunken, lazy, asshole husband she had turned me off and I lost all desire and stayed limp.

It was a good thing, I had become too distracted with his mother and almost forgotten the real reason I was here. Lucas was usually in his room watching TV and sneaking beers from his father. I could see where this kids life was going right away. Suddenly I didn't feel so bad for wanting to kill him; it kind of felt justified since I was becoming to hate his father as well as him now. The last thing this world needs is another drunken asshole using up taxpayer money buying more booze and helping absolutely nobody else.

My mother started to wonder where the hell I was going all the time. She was usually pretty good about keeping out of my business and we hardly talked anymore. She kind of lived in her own world since my dad died but I knew she loved me and was concerned where I was all the time. I told her I had met a girl, and had been spending my time with her and my new friend from school. I didn't mention any names just in case she wanted to put two and two together later.

At first I felt guilty about lying to her but if I were to tell her that I was plotting a murder and making love to my hand outside his mother's window she would probably freak out so I left it alone. She seemed at ease with that and didn't bring it up again. I knew that so long as I kept doing well in school and stayed away from trouble with the law that she would be okay so I assured her I would and it wasn't brought up again.

X.

It seemed like their entire family had something against keeping their curtains closed, which made my job a whole lot easier. I was getting his entire pattern down now, every little bit of it. He went jogging about three times a week since a conversation I listened to through his window in which I could hear his mother pushing on about it telling him, "It's a good habit to get into while you're young, I'm not going to sit around and watch you let yourself go like your father." He agreed with her with little more than a nod and a grumble, so I waited.

Lucas decided to go for jogs around 6:30 pm. He would always wear a red windbreaker, an old brick red colored one and some gray jogging sweats with white shorts over them. He would also always wear his gray sweatband. I thought he looked pretty funny for the morning he was about to die. I laughed to myself and began following him. He started running down the street towards an intersection leading straight towards the school; it would be full of people during the school year because it was the way all the kids who walked to school would take.

He was going towards the school because behind it was an old bike path that stretched on for exactly one mile. It also ran behind our properties and it was a good spot to go for a measured run. It was also nice and private. I had been watching him for a couple of weeks now going on his runs and he never took any other ways than his usual route on the bike path because it was a full mile run so if he ran it to the end and back he had in two miles for the day.

I decided this time to follow behind him a ways and to my surprise I couldn't keep up for long at all, he was pulling away from me and my lungs soon felt like they were going to burst. I wasn't prepared for this part, I had concentrated so hard on watching what he did I forgot about the fact that I would have to keep up with him if I wanted to do anything to him on one of these morning runs. I started to feel a bit desperate; I wanted this to happen today but it seemed the longer I followed him, the more energy he seemed to get and he never slowed or stopped.

I had never jogged outside of school track before and realized all too soon that when your lungs start burning and your legs turn to jelly, it becomes damn near impossible to keep going. I had to stop and watch him jog off into the horizon; my heart was beating like horse hooves on a fast run. It was probably for the better, me being so sloppily out of shape I might have been seen by him or made a mistake without my full focus on the task at hand.

I decided that it was definitely time for me to start adding cardio to my workouts because that was pathetic. If I couldn't keep up with my prey, how could I hunt it? So I started following him every day. Jogging behind him far enough that I could dip out of sight quickly if he happened to look back, which he occasionally did. I was proud of myself. Within a couple of months I found myself able to follow him for the full two mile run he did and I found myself a little less out of breath each time. I had pushed through a lot of pain to get here though. My first few times ended with me barely able to catch a full breath of air and vomiting in the nearby grass, out of sight from Lucas. I was surprised that he didn't hear or see me, though in the end determination won over and my goal of keeping up was accomplished.

I decided to attack on a Saturday. I was getting healthier and feeling stronger every day. I was also tired of having that damn nightmare every night and I was completely convinced that it would stop if I would just kill someone. It was driving me crazy. At the very least I wanted not to have the same dream every night. I was tired of waiting for it. The anticipation was too much and the longer I waited, the more I was convinced I was wasting my time. I could barely contain my excitement any longer, I found myself walking around with a huge secret and a half hard dick all the time now just thinking about how crazy I was about to get.

I know he had seen a couple of the sideways glances I had given him and the more afraid he looked, the more he looked like prey to me. So, that Saturday as he went jogging, I waited for him in a solitary spot in the trees along the bike path. I could see him coming and I felt my heart trying to beat through my chest. He was literally breathing some of his last breaths.

I gripped the knife I was holding so tightly that my hands turned albino white and I had to physically pry my fingers open. I realized that I had forgotten some kind of gloves to avoid having fingerprints on anything. *Oh well... there's no time now.* I waited until he came right up next to me and I pounced from behind the tree, aiming to plunge the knife deep into his neck, spewing forth life in a red sea of hot ooze that I had grown more than accustomed to from my dreams.

But everything went wrong.

I was so nervous and focused on the task at hand, that I didn't notice one of the roots of the tree sticking out of the ground right where I tried jumping out. I tripped over it feeling the same as when Lucas had pushed me before after tripping me and fell to the ground way harder than I probably should have. I fell flat on my face right in front of him. The knife slipped out of my hand as I fell trying to put my arms out in front of me but luckily I didn't impale myself, it landed flat and I landed right on top of it.

Lucas stopped almost with a skid looking at me, eyes wide with fear. His look slowly changed to something that was more of a cross between anger and fear. He kind of looked like a cornered animal for a second minus the bared teeth and foamy drool. I think just then the desperation in his fear took over because before I could get to my feet, he proceeded to kick the living shit out of me making sure I wasn't going to easily get up. I was just trying to block the barrage of kicks from him and starting to fail, losing my breath and wondering if I had a cracked rib or two? When I wasn't breathing right anymore, he finally stopped kicking at me, running away at double the speed as before.

I was pissed. I had just taken a pretty good kicking and I knew I would have to pay for that tomorrow but I still managed to get up and pick the knife up and run after him. We were near the woods connecting between our places and I knew nobody could see what was going on. With plenty of acres between properties, neighbors seeing or hearing anything wasn't a worry in my mind. He screamed "Help!" as I gained on him, surprised at how fast the adrenalin coursing through my veins was allowing me to run after I had been kicked like that. Before I could reach him he had reached his house. I trailed behind him about 100 feet, Close enough to have heard the back door of his place lock and I felt a sinking in the pit of my stomach. I was not going to let this happen.

It was him and his father at the house. When he went inside, I heard him yelling, "This crazy kid from school I used to beat up just jumped out from behind a tree and tried to stab me!"

To my amusement, his father actually got mad at him. "You're telling me that you didn't fuck him up and take his knife away, how is he supposed to learn never to mess with you!?!" I could hear the slaps and punches laid on Lucas as he said his words. I could hear Lucas starting to cry and trying to excuse his actions, but his father wasn't having it. I hid behind the little shed out of sight just in case his father came out or something, when I heard the door fling open. His father threw him down the steps and into the yard. "Get out there and teach him a lesson boy and don't come back without that knife." With a drunken sneer his father turned around and slammed the door shut.

I almost felt sorry for Lucas. Having a father like that has got to suck the blackest of assholes there is. Then I remembered how he once fucked up a kid whose father had just died, calling him a faggot, telling him that it was good his father was dead so he didn't have to take blame for raising such a waste of space. He even suggested that he watch his mom closely or she might kill herself to get away from him. I quickly stopped feeling pity for him, his dad may be a piece of shit but it still takes a real worthless human being to say things like that to a weak grieving boy.

Lucas was looking around frantically. He was in a panic searching for any sign of me, but I was deliberately where he couldn't see me. "WHERE ARE YOU, PUSSY?!" he yelled between his frightened and desperate deep breaths. I could see from my vantage point, a single booger running down his face as he started to circle the yard trying to be sneaky, but I was watching him.

"COME OUT COME OUT SO I CAN KICK THE SHIT OUT OF YOU SOME MORE!" he screamed as he shook his breathing becoming faster now. He got to the back side of the shed where I was hiding, watching him. I was waiting until just the right moment when I would see his shadow letting me know he was close. When I saw it I took my opportunity, jumping out and jamming the knife down at him. He let out a quick gasp as he was trying to say no but he could only get the "n-n-n" sound out. He was scared as hell right now. I don't even know if he thought about screaming for his dad, he just locked up trying to stop my hand. He got lucky again as I thrust the knife down, some sort of adrenalin allowed him to see and catch my hand but this time, he tripped over the concrete the shed was sitting on and fell down with my full weight landing on top of him.

The knife had plunged directly into his face, to the hilt, a full eight inches. It had also pinned one of his hands to him as he tried to block it. He shook a little bit, his body having a 10 second or so epileptic fit, I could see his left eye through a couple of spread fingers on his hand that was pinned to his face widen for a few seconds and then relax. Then he just stopped.

I lay there for a minute just staring at him; I couldn't believe I had actually done it. I had dreamed about this moment since I first thought of it and now it was finally done. I looked down at him and he almost looked surreal, a rendition from an artist's mind maybe, but no more.

Things like this usually didn't happen in real life and it felt a little fake to me. Then I remembered the feeling of the knife plunging into his face with all that weight behind it. I had felt it happen.

I know he was dead now but, the look on his face was almost too perfect, almost too good of a picture to be real life. His eye was still wide open. The knife had missed both of his eyeballs and had actually penetrated his face between the bridge of his nose, and his right eye through the palm of his hand about where his middle fingers knuckle was. You couldn't see any of the blade of the knife anymore.

I leaned forward to hold his head in my hands and look into his eye to see if I could spot something as his brain died. His right eye was totally covered. The left eye was still working and I watched it's pupil grow so big it almost made his brown eye black and it seemed to dim, there was a barely noticeable flicker and then, nothing. Just an empty stare, forever looking at nothing, I knew that there would be no saving him.

It was a beautiful moment that I wish could have lasted a while longer, but I heard the front door open and Lucas' father stuck out his head and yelled, "BOY, WHERE YOU AT NOW?" There was no answer. "IF YOU DON'T ANSWER ME, I'M GONNA KICK YOUR ASS TWICE, JUST FOR GOOD MEASURE!" When there was still no answer he came stumbling outside and down the steps. I hid behind a tree next to the shed and began to panic a little. If he comes any closer, he was going to see Lucas body! It didn't take but a few more steps and he looked right at his sons lifeless body lying on the ground before him with a knife handle buried to the hilt in his face.

The last thing he had done was yelled at him and beat him for not being strong enough. To my surprise he dropped to his knees right there and started to cry. First softly as if he were trying to build up the tears to be able to cry, the numbness from drinking probably having killed that long ago. Then he started bawling, heavy tears.

I was curious at the fact he didn't even look around in his drunken stupor to see if anyone was around. "I'M SO SORRY SON. WHAT HAVE I DONE? WAKE UP SON, PLEASE!" Between tears of despair and the drunken haze, he sounded like he almost believed his son was going to get up and be just fine. He leaned down and hugged his dead son close to him. He had blood all over him now. I was curious how someone could be so careless but he was definitely two sheets to the wind long before he came out here.

I was becoming uncomfortable standing in one spot for so long and tried to shift my weight to put it on the other foot. A small branch under my feet snapped with a loud crack. I heard myself gasp and his dad turned towards the noise.

He realized who was there. "YOU!" He screamed and started towards me. I didn't know what to do. His father no longer had human looking eyes. They were black in the middle and all red where they were once white. He was pissed! I knew that he was going to kill me very painfully and probably slowly if he caught me. He was a full one hundred pounds heavier than I was my meager 135 pounds and he was pretty drunk, which meant that he probably wouldn't even feel pain. For the first time since this adventure in murder, I was a little scared. I was probably only getting out of here in a body bag or a police car.

I was able to snap out of my panic long enough to see one opportunity directly on the side of me. Lying on the ground in front of me was one of those old metal rakes with a wooden handle that was no longer rounded out. It had been broken off a couple inches probably from this guy beating shit with it and had sharp points that could make a decent weapon. In the second I had before he reached me, I stomped on the metal teeth hard enough to make the rake come up towards him and he hit it with the full weight of his body at tackling speed. He hit it at an angle which made the wooden end of the rake enter his mouth. That didn't stop the drunken bull rush and instead of stopping he fell into it with all of his weight. His body wasn't able to just fall forward onto the ground because of the forked edge bracing against the ground. It all happened so fast and he was so drunk he probably hit it with double the force he should have.

It caught him just right to hoist his body off the ground by his mouth before busting through the back of his head, completely impaling his drunken head through with the rake handle. It was like he shot himself with a bullet, or like he was a vampire who had staked himself. His weight tried to let his body fall forward, but the flat part of the rake would let it go no further and he slowly slid down the rake handle bloodying up the entire length of wood until his head was resting on the part of the rake that connects the metal part to the stick. The metal of the rake propped up his head at a very uncomfortable looking angle and the handle was still sticking straight up. It looked as if his body had become a stable base, like one that would hold up a Christmas tree. Imagine that present under the tree on a white Christmas.

I just lay there stunned now. I wanted to kill Lucas... that much was planned on but this second death; that was like a bonus two-for-one special murder.

I started shaking uncontrollably. It was similar to the feeling some get when they first kill a deer, like a sort of adrenalin. I felt good, I felt above reproach, I felt above the law and I felt... panicked.

I had to make sure there were no fingerprints, or any prints at all, shoe or otherwise. I tried to remember if I had spit or anything anywhere and then I remembered the window. It had been weeks since I visited her so I doubted I had to worry about that, it had also been raining heavily a few times since then. I thought about what I would do with the bodies. The thought of course came of eating them, but at the moment I couldn't imagine trying to eat someone, I could barely imagine cutting them up realistically.

Lucas was lying on his back, the knife in his hand in his face. He had stopped bleeding long ago now. His father was lying on his stomach, the rake handle protruding from the back of his head and sticking up in the air. They were probably about ten feet apart from each other at the moment. I suddenly got a great idea that would have impressed me, had I not been pressed for time.

I did what any logical thinking person who had just killed two people would do. First, I opened the shed. Right on the inside of the door was a pair of leather gloves. I used them first to wipe the prints off of the knife handle and then to get a better grip. I turned the rake little by little by the metal end in a circle, lifting his fathers head up a couple of times so it wasn't stuck on it. I moved it a full 180 degrees until it was facing the other way. I lifted and carried Lucas body a few feet until I could get his father's right hand around the knife in his son's face and then moved him back where he was, trying to be as careful as I could to make it look normal.

I wiped away most of the footprints of mine in the dirt that I could find and threw some pine needles and loose dirt down to better help hide any that might be left. When I was satisfied, I took off into the woods and went back to my house. As soon as I got to my yard, I threw up for real.

I didn't throw up quite as bad as I had in my reoccurring nightmares but, I threw up nonetheless.

I looked into the mirror before my shower. I stood there for a good twenty minutes, staring into the eyes of a new killer, then washed the blood away in the shower like so many sins. I probably took a shower double the length of my normal but I just felt like I couldn't get the blood all off of me, I didn't really have much on me, his hand had blocked some of the blood spatter from spraying me but I was definitely going to have to burn those gloves. I didn't have to worry about the knife either; it was from a dollar store anyone could have bought one. I hoped I had remembered everything else important that might matter. I was ready to sleep before too long, something about murder had made me extra tired tonight and I fell asleep quickly. The nightmares didn't come again for a long time.

XI

That was the true beginning of my criminal career. There were those kids who had seen what I had become towards Lucas but I don't think that they would ever actually entertain the idea that it could have been me that did something so horrific as kill him and his father. If the thought had crossed any of their minds I never so much as heard a whisper of it. The Police said that this was an obvious homicide by Lucas' drunken, crazed father. His mother had come home and found them after her shift that night.

I knew the moment that she found them because I could hear her screams echoing across the forest where I was sitting in my back yard. It was a bit muffled due to the distance but there was no mistaking what those painful sounds of woe were. They continued for a while and then suddenly stopped, making me think she had maybe killed herself. I was a bit concerned until I heard the sirens in the distance.

I didn't want this for Lucas mother. In fact, I had sort of become infatuated with her lately. As sick as it made me feel I wanted to go to her and try and console her, but I knew that it was a fantasy in my own head and that she would probably never go for it. I didn't know if it was some sort of subconscious reaction to the fact I had just killed her family or what it was, but when I sat there listening to her wailings of despair, I felt more attracted to her than ever, and my thoughts of her began to consume me. What she needed was some kind of closure; people don't tend to dwell on things when they have an acceptable story to quench those burning questions in their minds, allowing them to move on.

She would immediately draw the conclusion that her husband had done it and had accidentally killed himself, which was what I was going for. She attested that he was a horribly abusive man and had beaten Lucas and her many times. That was more than enough motive for the police. They already knew that she was working when her husband and son were killed and the scenario seemed to fit the suspicions. Lucas had said the wrong thing to his drunken father one last time and good old Dad let his alcoholic rage take over, going too far this time and killing his son.

Their story about the incident was that the Lucas stormed out of the house afraid that his father would beat him again, or worse. Lucas father ran after him eventually catching him by the shed where he stabbed his son directly through the hand and face when he put his hand up to try and protect himself from his fathers rage. Lucas had in fact been beaten right before he had died, so it was actually perfect. His father's hands were also bruised, making for an easy open shut abuse case. He also had a pretty high blood alcohol content of .420 which was beyond the point where normal people would have passed out or slipped into a coma.

The police surmised that when he was trying to move Lucas body, he had stumbled onto the rake making it stand up on the forks, then they thought he had drunkenly tripped over it in a twisted loop of fate and unable to stop himself in his fall, impaled his head on the rakes jagged broken end sliding down the entire length of it. It was chalked up to karma with a lot of laughs around the police station. To the cops it was just another drunk, abusive father who got what he deserved.

I couldn't believe it. I had actually gotten away with murder.

I went back to school in a daze, mindlessly going through my classes. The teachers weren't very impressive right now. They were more concerned with the awful story that they had to portray for us in hopes that none of the kids that were abused in their own personal lives were feeling suicidal. Kids would cry together. Not because they missed this asshole everyone thought was murdered by his drunken father, but because it touched them on a personal level that it could have been any of them. They realized that at any moment, at any age, any one of them could die. It reminded them about the precious quality of life and that life was fragile. It never promises we will live forever, our lives can last as little as one more day, or they could last more than a hundred years. The only thing that is certain is that one day… we will all die, some much sooner than others.

Lucas father must be be rolling over in his grave. One minute he's sitting in his living room trying to teach his son to be a man so he could finish his show in peace, then the commercial break hits, and he's dead shortly after his son. He would have been fine I'm sure had he not been such a drunk, we would probably be in each other's places. I probably got lucky that he didn't kill me. When he came barreling at me I felt a huge wave of panic sweep over me. I wanted nothing more than to just shit myself and teleport to a safe place where this man would never be able to find me. The look in his eyes more than said he was about to strangle me and tenderize my body until I was nothing more than a bag of bloody mush. Things didn't turn out the way he planned though, but that's what you get for being weak and unable to control something as debilitating as alcohol.

All alcohol did for him from what I had seen is made him a complete asshole and tear his family apart. I would never have picked Lucas to kill if he had never become such a worthless abuser all on his own merit. If his dad was more in control of his alcohol, he and his son might still be alive. I had seen him sober one time at the county fair last year and he seemed almost nice. He was going through detox at the time and promised he was a new man. I guess he lied.

Ultimately, it was his inability to move soberly that brought about his horrid, painful downfall. What a way to go, sliding all the way to the bottom of the rake face-first like that. I wonder if he felt anything by then or if the alcohol was his salvation for once in his life. That had to be the worst headache ever felt by someone if he was alive all the way until he reached the bottom. I had to feel a little sad for the guy, at least for a moment.

Who I really felt bad for though, was Lucas' poor mother. If there was anyone in this whole situation who deserved a little sympathy, it was definitely her. I think I might have to stop by sometime and give her my condolences. I'm sure she might like a warm shoulder to spill her sweet tears on. I wanted to at least stop by tonight and see her through the window, like before. When I got to her house later that night though it was all cordoned off with yellow tape, from the edge of the yard I could see that she had all the shades drawn for the first time that I had ever seen. I wasn't going to be able to see her tonight.

Just the thought of her soft skin, her full perfect breasts, and the tears running down her sweet face as she cried was enough to start the goose bumps forming on my arms. I wanted to make her feel better so badly but instead, I walked back to my house to have another night of dreamless slumber.

XII.

Two years later.

I woke from a dead sleep to a repetitive banging noise that sounded like it was coming from downstairs in the kitchen. I got out of bed with a heavy sigh and sleepily walked down the stairs hearing bang after bang around the corner at the bottom of the stairs. I wished that I had a bat or other weapon of some kind, but I had nothing around me at the moment and I was already halfway to where the banging was coming from so I just kept on going. I walked into the kitchen and I could see the reflections of lightning flashing on the walls, ceiling and floor of the dining room through the window. The banging seemed to stop as soon as I had reached the bottom of the staircase, but I was sure it had come from in the kitchen somewhere.

I looked outside the window and I could see the shadow of a humongous tree next to my kitchen. I couldn't remember for the life of me if I actually had a tree out there, but this one did seem familiar to me. I knew I had seen it before, I just couldn't remember from where. Suddenly I heard a heavy tapping behind me coming from across the room and as quickly as I turned around a gigantic hand like tree branch busted through the window and grabbed me ripping me through the window and part of the wall.

I was now a muscular 18 years old. I began acquiring and lifting weights vowing to never let another kid get bullied on my watch. I wanted to become the scariest I could become. Nobody challenged me anyways, it seemed that I had done it, I had taken the glue of bullying which was Lucas, and I had melted it away ending the abuse for good. It felt great, I hadn't felt the desire to kill since I had taken the lives of Lucas and his father, but once the tree held me in front of his face again I remembered it all just as if it had been yesterday. I had a sinking feeling in the pit of my stomach. I hadn't dreamt about this tree in so long that it had begun fading from my memory. I would never forget it; it just wasn't on the forefront of my mind anymore. I was lifted up to stare into the black hole in it and I heard the booming voice from the seemingly distant past once again; only this time I wasn't afraid of it.

"THE BLOOD MAKES IT REAL!" The loud voice boomed from the deep darkness in front of me. I could feel the voice vibrate in what seemed to be every cell in my being, shaking me to the core. The tree then proceeded to stuff me into itself again with its enormous and strong branch arms, the impossible darkness surrounding me all at once. I turned around quickly and although I was just put into this hole, I couldn't see out of the other side already.

I was instantly surrounded by absolute darkness just as before. I was once again weightless, as if the air itself was surrounding me perfectly on all sides, holding my entire weight from all angles at the same time. Just as before, a television like picture came on. I was curious this time and I tried to touch the image only to find that I couldn't, it was like a hologram in the middle of nothingness. I remember thinking how cool that would be in my living room. It had the ultimate picture; there was a perfect quality that zoomed in wherever you wanted to look the most.

A picture started to show up and I saw who I could only assume to be me but I barely recognized myself. I was sitting inside of a 7 by 3 foot wide rectangular shaped metal tub, surrounded by what appeared to be human organs and I was covered in blood. When I say covered, I mean I was completely covered from head to toe. I didn't have a spot on my body that wasn't red. The only non-red color on me was from the whites of my eyes as I looked forward with an intense stare and the flesh of my lips as I licked them in what seemed to be pure ecstasy. The blood that was there was thinner and smeared in a circle where my tongue had gone over it.

I willed the view right up in front of my own face on this screen for a nice close up shot. My eyes were scary looking; I seemed completely at peace to be covered in someone else's insides. My stare was deep like I was in some sort of trance almost but it also had a very resolved look on it. It felt like the blood had healed whatever might have ailed my body and was now giving me powers beyond that of a mere human. The look on my face was much like the one I must have had at the first moment I realized I had gotten away with murder. The kind of look a pet cat might give after slaughtering a mouse in your honor, kind of an eyes half-closed confidence to it. The same look Muhammad Ali gets before he fights an opponent, that look that says "I know I'm going to win."

I could look anywhere that I wanted to in this holographic vision I was watching unfold before me. As I stood up and turned around, so did the screen until I had a 360 degree view surrounding me. If it was too dark in a corner I could will the disembodied light to shine like a spotlight so that I could see in detail anything I wanted. I looked above my future bloody self and I could see a body strung up above my head. I could see it was a big guy, probably around 35 years old, with a gigantic slash on his midsection that spilled his blood and guts all over my future body in the huge tub. I could see the man's stomach and intestines; they had slipped into a comfortable circle around my blood soaked body and even looked to be steaming a bit.

I was suddenly glad this tree didn't have smell-o-vision like it does for seeing things. Future me had slashed the guy open. The look on the man's face told me that he had still been alive through the ordeal; I know that the body can survive for a while with its organs outside of itself. His mouth was forever stuck in a terrified frown which from upside down made It look more like a strange smile. His nostrils were filled with blood. His eyes had rolled up into his head and since he was upside down it looked as if he was looking at the floor in great pain.

The whites of his eyes were blood red. It looked like damn near every blood vessel in them had popped. He had a bloated black and blue face streamed with dried blood and there were trails where he had pissed himself and urine had flowed down his body culminating on his face before falling into the tub below. I'm sure there were tears in his hair; I couldn't tell if he had been crying, he was too streaked with blood and urine to allow me to see clearly. It definitely didn't look like it felt any sort of good.

I watched in awe as future I stepped out of the tub with his blood soaked body. I had gained quite a bit of weight from the look of it and looked to be in my early twenties now. I had a lot more muscle now and I couldn't imagine I ever got picked on anymore. I watched as future me walked to the shower to rinse off all of the blood and entrails. The place I was in was definitely homemade. It looked to be set up to butcher animals and cut them into whatever size steaks might be needed. It even had a shower for cleaning up when the work became too bloody.

It had the tub set right in the middle of a large area for bleeding the animals where he had been soaking in blood and organs. There was an area leading back towards the showering area on the right, which was just a simple stand up surrounded by stucco-like wall you might see at a swimming pool or in a community shower. There was also a room to the left of the showers, it was around 15 by 20 feet long and had a table with cutlery of all sorts and various other equipment on it. I could sense it was for cutting up bodies by the knife and saw collections in here. It was surprisingly clean though, I recalled with a hint of dislike since I would have to become tidy to make this kind of future happen.

I couldn't believe how built and crazy I had become. If this was indeed how I turned out, I had become exactly what I was aiming for now, scary. I saw myself grab a large knife from the kitchen and go back out to the tub and cut a large square section out of his back an inch thick, a foot long and 6 inches wide before walking back out of the room. I went to follow and watch what happened next, suspecting cannibalism and it suddenly got very dark around me again, I couldn't seem to make the light or the vision come back on. I heard a loud sound fill the air that sounded much like white noise.

I was suddenly thrown from the tree back into my house and I felt my body in a snap pulled back up the stairs into my bedroom by an unseen entity. I looked down and I could see my body lying in bed and I had the thought that I might be dead. I was about to start panicking when I was thrown again, this time into my body. I awoke instantly sitting up with a gasp and looked around noticing that my vision was definitely a little bit different than what I was just seeing. It seemed to be a bit brighter and more detailed when I was out of my body; I also didn't see so many weird colors now.

Interesting, I thought as I lay my head back down. I hadn't had a dream about the tree for a long time. To me it meant that it was time to kill again, I didn't mind, I had to admit I liked the feeling of power I got from ending a life. This time it would have to be more smoothly planned out, no more accidental deaths, no more mistakes or unplanned events happening. I lay there for a while smiling, thinking of murder scenarios before drifting off to sleep again. It was adventure time once again.

XIII.

I woke up the next morning feeling pretty good all things considered. It wasn't like I had the compunction to murder someone else, I just knew that things would be like they were before if I didn't. I wasn't really in the mood to have that repetitive nightmare for months on end or however long it was going to take. They have given people the death sentence for the kinds of things I had done. I was going to just accept it and deal with it as I needed to.

The dream said it was time to kill again from what I understood of it and this time I would make no mistakes. I had gotten away with it before somehow, although I'm sure there were things that were overlooked at the crime scene. I just got lucky that they had a messed up relationship in the first place and the story was so easily accepted. There was no guarantee that the next time I had a victim in my hands, I was going to be able to create a scenario that was so readily accepted on the spot, it wasn't something I could ever afford to try again, I had to be much more careful next time.

I started to watch people everywhere I went. I wanted to find the most deserving of prospects trying to decide who to kill was harder than I thought it would be. I found myself examining my mental state more closely than I expected and I realized that I was thinking obsessively about whom my next victim might be. I thought maybe another abusive father, or maybe another bully that likes to pick on the weaker people, like Lucas. Whomever it would be this time needed to really deserve it, I didn't want to murder just anyone. I wanted to find the most deserving of people, but then who deserves to be murdered, was it really up to me to decide?

It absolutely was, I realized the simple fact that I even had to ask myself that question proved that I was capable of making choices of such a grand magnitude. Maybe it was partly due to the fact that my future self seemed to be so confident in what he had done and I couldn't imagine that I would have changed that much from where I was now. Right now there were people that I wouldn't blink an eye at murdering if I thought it through thoroughly. I felt like a vigilante from the Wild West gun slinging cowboy days. Someone would become wanted and the sheriff would offer a bounty for them. Anyone had a chance to bring them in and collect a reward usually dead or alive. I felt like that anyone, except that I would be bringing nobody in. I would be erasing them from the face of the earth. There would be no bringing them in alive.

It was going to be a daunting task but I was determined to find someone. The nightmare had come back again and again the last few nights and I didn't want to live through that again. They had changed now in that they were showing me different things. I was beginning to see more of the logical side to murder. Firstly, I didn't just murder in the future and leave it all behind. Right now there was no way I was going to be able to bring meat home and try it like in my dreams; the thought gagged me a little in fact. But I was going to have to start thinking logically about not leaving evidence around or this would be the shortest career in killing there ever was.

I would look at the people walking by me on the streets and try to gauge how I felt about them, if they were worthy of my murderous impulses or not. I saw a fat balding man in a white t-shirt and bulging blue jeans that looked almost as if half of his body were turned around and facing the wrong way than the rest. I caught myself grinning as I thought about killing him just to put him out of his misery. I could blame it on one of seven deadly sins, gluttony. He looked like he was having a hard time breathing and he had his mouth hanging open.

As he walked past me he glanced at me long enough for me to look right into his eyes. I could see nothing evil in them; he was rather innocent looking actually and had kind eyes. I tried to restrain the look of pity that I could feel forming on my face, averting my gaze as I walked past him. That's not the kind of person I wanted to become, the one who just starts killing indiscriminately with little or no real reason. *I wasn't that kind of person was I?*

I began walking across town letting my mind wander. I walked past a house that had a group of Mexicans standing outside; each one had a beer in their hand and bloodshot dark eyes. I could see the nonchalance in their eyes and knew that none of them really cared about a whole lot of anything right now. One of them was laughing saying something in Spanish to his buddies and they all narrowed their eyes and laughed as if he just told them he had been fucking a virgin and she had gotten blood on his dick, so he wiped it on the curtains of her living room. He had probably raped someone at some point in his life but that was pure speculation on my part and I wanted to know for sure whether or not they deserved it. I suddenly thought of a great way to do that.

My friend Curtis had a cop for a father. One time when I was a bit younger I was at his house and we went on the internet. Curtis signed in under his father's name to the police database where he could look up criminals and run names and addresses on people. He wasn't really supposed to do it but his father could and he didn't really care as long as his son didn't bring attention to the fact he was on there. His father showed him the site often when he was growing up trying to teach him what NOT to grow up to be. He told me it was cool and that we could look at it whenever I was at his house.

It had been more than a year now since I last hung out with him, but he still lived at his parents place. I didn't imagine he would be moving out until he was in his 30's. His mother was just too coddling of him and his father does whatever his mother wants him to. I was a little worried since I had killed two people and his father was a cop. An irrational fear was trying to tell me that he might be able to see the lies on my face when he looked at me.

His father was actually one of those pretty cool cops that didn't ever bring his work attitude to people when he was off duty. Not to mention that any friend of his son's he considered to be a friend of his. Curtis had a hard time making friends; he was already a weird kid and he had pretty much everything he wanted, but there was always something off about him. If I wasn't the killer around here I could easily see it being him one day.

It was pure accident that I even met him in the first place. I was out riding my bike, I was 13 years old. I was bored out of my skull and looking for something to do when I saw this kid leaning out of his window talking to himself like he was a fighter pilot. He was holding a glider plane and shouting about taking out the enemy target and answering himself promising that he would. He launched the glider out the window and I watched it as it looped up, did a full backflip and started soaring away.

I thought it was a goner but just then it turned on another wind current and started coming back my direction. Before I could do a thing I noticed that it was coming directly at me. It hit me full in the face bloodying and fattening my lip almost instantly. Curtis came running down stairs and outside. At first I wanted to be mad at him but I couldn't because I knew it wasn't really his fault.

"I'm so sorry man!" He exclaimed a bit out of breath from running all the way downstairs to come and see if I was alright.

I could feel my lip pulsating as if it had a heart of its own. "It's alright man; I know you didn't mean to, it's just my dumb luck though." I laughed.

My laughing seemed to ease his overly anxious state and he relaxed holding out his hand. "I'm Curtis".

I grabbed his hand and shook it but before I could tell him my name he started in again, he was a hyper little guy. "Do you want to come up and play some games with me? I have a Nintendo and all sorts of stuff to do."

"Sure, why not? I replied and went upstairs with him. If nothing else I could tend to my swollen lip. He showed me his arsenal of video games and toys and I was blown away, he had everything a kid could want, almost every game, as well as all the newest toys that were out. He had collected them from his family who wanted to help him feel better about his inability to make friends. It was a nice gesture on their part, but I would later learn from him that it was a painful slap in the face to get the new toys and have nobody to play with them with. It gets lonely playing by yourself all the time, I knew that firsthand. It was something I was going to have to get used to but as far as seeing my friend Curtis tomorrow I needed to rectify not visiting in such a long time. At least he hadn't called me either, so I couldn't feel too bad. I was going to have to give him a call tomorrow.

XIV.

"Hello?" Came the age old familiar voice that I had been missing for too long now.

"Curtis man, what's up? Long time no talk to!" I said.

He knew who it was on the phone right away. "Oh hey man I wondered what happened to you. I figured you forgot about me by now." He laughed a bit uneasily, I could tell that he was glad I called but he seriously thought I had forgotten about him.

"Naw, I could never forget about you man, I just had a lot going on. I haven't really talked to anyone for a while; I just wanted to deal my shit on my own. It was kind of a mental thing but I'm better now! So how's it been with you?" I asked quickly trying to change the subject.

"Well you know, it's the same thing around here all the time, I have gotten used to it you know. So what's up bro? I'm glad you called" He sounded genuinely pleased to hear from me.

"Nothing real significant I guess," I lied, "Just wondering what you have been up to after all this time, you know. We haven't hung out in such a long time and I'm about ready to blow my top if I don't get some away time from myself soon." I'm sure he could almost hear my smile over the phone.

"Yeah that sounds good man; I suppose that you could come over tomorrow night if you want." He said. "Tonight's not really a good night. My dad's fighting with my mom and it sounds pretty serious."

"That sucks, what happened?" I asked.

"Well apparently this junkie guy who is dating one of my mom's best friends like beat the ever loving shit out of her and put her in the hospital and shit. Now my mom keeps telling him to be a real cop and go shoot the guy. My dad told her that he wants to but he can't because there isn't enough evidence to prove the guy was guilty and her friend won't talk about it."

"Damn, that's some deep shit man, yeah tomorrow probably would be better I guess." I said.

"Now my mom is freaking out on him for always choosing to be on the side of the law." He laughed. "Good grief I mean he is a cop for shit's sake. He tried to get a warrant for him but it failed since my mom's friend won't say anything against him. Her boyfriend said he got home and she was unconscious and the door was wide open. They don't exactly live in the best neighborhood but my mother's friend had told her the night before that he was always hitting her and like forcing her to do whatever he wanted her to all the time.

She called my mom like an hour before her hospital trip saying he was totally out of control this time. He had choked her out and let his dealer fuck her in her ass for some more dope, whatever that means. So she wakes up to this stranger fucking her in her ass, and when he finishes and leaves her boyfriend beats her for fucking someone else! I've been hearing her yelling at my dad about it for a while now. She doesn't even do drugs but for some reason she was too scared to leave the guy. Now she's been sitting in the hospital all fucked up like that, he's a real piece of shit you know?"

I did know…and my blood was already getting warmer. This was sounding like exactly what I had been waiting for. This was someone who wouldn't be missed by anyone and would be less of a murder and more of a cleansing for the fucked up world we live in. I asked him, "Who is this guy?"

"It's this guy named Shane who lives in this blue house on the corner of Spencer and Fourth Avenue down in the ghetto side of town. All he does is sell speed all day and get high I guess, I don't know why someone like him gets to live and then people like her get put in the hospital."

"Yeah I know. That's pretty shitty man I hope she's going to be okay. The cops did nothing to the guy?"

"Nope, he was smoking meth like two hours before he beat her ass and she was talking to my mom on the phone. It's pretty much all that he does from what I hear so I'm sure he's just partying it up getting high while she's gone too."

That kind of thing makes me sick. I'm not about beating a woman ever, especially bad enough to put her in the hospital, but to celebrate and act like it was okay after she is laid up in the E.R? Unacceptable. I guess that I had some planning to do.

"Hey I'll call you tomorrow before I come over alright?"

"Alright, sounds good, bye."

As soon as we hung up I packed up a bag, grabbed my keys and walked out the door. I got on my bike and rode it to the corner of Spencer and 4th and sure enough there was a blue house there just like Curtis had said there was. I rode my bike over to a nice dark spot across the road big enough to hide me and my bike behind it. I pulled my backpack off of my back and opened it to reveal some nice comfortable black gloves which I put on before doing anything else. Every video I had seen inside the tree I had been wearing gloves, which I liked. Besides, it made no sense to get my fingerprints on anything. I decided not to worry too much about planning this one either, he was a drug addict and I already had an idea about how I would go about this.

First though, I needed to survey the scene and make sure that things were going to work out to my advantage. I stayed behind the large bush at a vantage point that I could see the blue house without being seen by anyone else. I thought I was going to be shit out of luck because all the curtains were drawn shut and I couldn't see inside. There were random shadows of what must have been a lamp, and another of maybe a shelf of some sort, I couldn't really tell. I watched closely for a few minutes trying to see any shadows moving inside and after a bit, to my relief, I did. It got even better because he came outside.

From what I could tell having never done any kinds of drugs at this point in my life, (unless you count adrenaline) he was definitely high. His eyes were far too open and he kept sniffling and running his hand down his face as if he were trying to wipe off some kind of sticky invisible goo or something. At other times it looked like he was trying to clear cobwebs off of his face and he constantly moved his jaw back and forth while his eyes remained bugged out of his head. I couldn't tell exactly what it was that he was searching for but apparently he found it.

I saw him pick up something light colored and sort of rectangular and turn around and walk back inside. I was absolutely sure I had found the right place, this guy with his shrunken dehydrated head and wiry frame looked like just the kind of asshole that would put his brutality on a female's fragility. He was dressed like a character from an 80's movie. He wore leather cutoff jacket and jeans with holes in them. He had a chain holding his wallet to his pants. His hair was unkempt and messy and he looked like he hadn't showered in a week or more. I put my hood up and secured it a bit, left my bag and bike and walked across the street dressed in an all-black sweat suit and cheap pair of black shoes that I could just dispose of afterwards so I wouldn't have to worry about footprints.

I crept as stealthily as a ninja into his backyard. He had the curtains drawn around the back side of the house too, but they were only partly shut. There were random parts of the shades open, and a couple of the actual blind pieces were bent from what I figured was excessive peeking. I had never done meth but I had seen a lot of people on it. It didn't really look appealing. I could see him in the chair in the kitchen and from this viewpoint I could see what he had picked up. It looked like a clear baggie about two inches by probably three inches tall, filled with some clear quartz or crystal looking rocks. I figure that must be the speed, I didn't know for sure but I had heard it was clear looking and people called them, "shards".

I watched as he pulled out a dirty old looking spoon and from what I could see black as hell on the bottom. He put a few of the quartz looking rocks in there. Then he put some water in the spoon with it and started mixing it around seemingly trying to melt them down. Apparently the rocks didn't melt fast enough for him because he pulled out a lighter and proceeded to put the flame underneath the spoon. The rocks melted down quickly and he mixed it a little more with the end of an unopened needle.

He pulled a Q-tip out of a box he had sitting on the table in front of him. He then pulled little pieces of cotton off and rolled them into a little ball, put them in the spoon then sucked the liquid from the melted rocks up into a syringe and proceeded to tie off his upper arm and slap the spot in the crease of your arm where you would normally have blood drawn at the doctor. He pointed the needle into the air and flicked it a couple of times before he was satisfied. He stuck the needle into a bulging vein that had popped up from the rubber piece tied around his upper arm and pulled the pusher part back until blood showed up and mixed with his drugs and then he emptied it in his arm.

I watched as in a few seconds he went from looking merely anxious to looking wide eyed and twitchy. Then his eyes grew wider than I could have thought possible and I thought he looked like he was going to die. The color on his face had paled immensely. He tried to stand up and immediately stumbled backwards into the wall of the kitchen busting the drywall in a large oval shape. He started shaking and I could actually see what looked like steam coming off his neck. I thought that was impossible but he was sweating horribly now. I thought maybe he had overdosed.

All of a sudden he lunged forward and in a long fast pounce reached the kitchen sink. He shoved the cold water on and immersed his head as far as he could under the cold water in one smooth motion. He was still shivering like he was in below freezing weather but the water seemed to be helping the steam from forming off of his neck anyways. I watched as his breathing became raspy and more desperate by the second. He was taking long fast breaths and I felt he might hyperventilate if he didn't stop.

I would be pissed if he died by his own hand because I wanted to kill him myself. I still had the picture of his girlfriend crying and screaming for him to stop and him continuing a relentless attack that eventually would put her in the hospital. He shut the water off and turned around, shaking much more vigorously now. His eyes were closed and his head was tilted back and he was taking long breaths like he just ran a mile and was trying to catch his breath. It didn't seem to be working for him and he sat down on the couch and tried just sitting still for a minute.

After about thirty seconds, he started flopping back and forth on the couch, each time with a loud exhale and he would shift his head to the side and put up his arms like he didn't know what to do with his body, much the same as a drunken spinning person who starts moving just to move, right before they start puking.

About four shifts left to right and right to left, he finally stopped and I could see his breathing becoming shallower. His eyes rolled up into his eyelids which were half shut and I saw the front of his pants darken, he had just pissed himself. He lurched forward and vomited, mostly yellow bile looking shit which is probably exactly what it was since speed freaks usually don't eat much. Then he just sat there for about five minutes hunched over like that before getting up and walking over to the sink again. He turned the water back on, using his hands to take a couple of drinks and wet his face. He was probably trying to rinse some of the sweat he had recently become soaked with. I was glad he was okay, at least until I get my hands on him. I sure hope he enjoyed almost dying, because I was about to finish the job.

XV.

I walked towards the door through the trashed yard after looking around carefully to make sure that nobody was around or just hidden from my view. It was pretty dark so I took my time. There was nobody, so I checked if the door was locked by turning the handle a little bit. It was unlocked, I turned the handle nice and slow, I didn't know if it would squeak or not. I was extra careful not to make any unnecessary noise but he had his head under the tap with the water on full blast so I doubted he could hear anything if he wanted to. When the knob turned as far as it would go I pushed to try and ease the door open.

Nothing, it was dead bolted. My heart was racing so fast I almost could hear it and then I had this anticlimactic moment. I was already here and nobody was around to witness anything that may happen, so I gave a quick police knock on the door. I could almost imagine the stupid look on his face as he looked at the door from inside unsure if anyone had really knocked or not. I imagined his eyes were bugged out as he tried to figure out whether or not to answer it. Apparently he wasn't too worried about who might show up because he opened the door right away. It took him a second more than it should have to focus on me but I had just watched him almost overdose so I wasn't surprised at all.

His initial look when his eyes caught up to the moment was one of anger as if he couldn't believe someone could be knocking at his door, but his look quickly turned to surprise. As I looked into his eyes, my rage hit me all at once and before I knew it I kicked him with a surprising strength dead in his chest knocking him backwards faster than he could react. He hit his old gas stove hard enough to knock the whole thing sideways but his body seemed to be made up of the same material as a super bouncy ball. I had to hold back a surprised gasp as he ricocheted off of the stove and came right back at me.

He was obviously much too high to remember how to do much else besides hold on, which kind of threw me for a loop because he was just fine when he battered the shit out of his woman. I attempted multiple times to get my hands around his neck and he kept grabbing and holding my wrists as if I would eventually get tired and all he had to do was wait it out.

He kept saying, "I don't know you, what the fuck are you doing, what do you want?" His wiry frame was trying to get me to leave the house but all he could accomplish was his feet sliding across the floor. I looked at him briefly during the struggle and he was looking at me cross-eyed. This really should have been much more of a fight but he was too high to know what was going on. This whole high, it seemed, wasn't a very enjoyable one.

This could have been an anti-drug commercial for him, if I didn't already have other plans. I finally got tired of him holding my wrists and decided to kick him in the shin, hard. Four, five, six times I counted before he finally let my wrists go and instead, grabbed his shin.

"Shit man, what did you do that for?" he screamed. I didn't answer him. Instead, I took his moment of confusion as an opportunity and ran towards him making sure to point to the left behind his head to make him look, which in his mental state, he did. When his head turned for a second I juked to the right and went behind him before he realized anything was off and put my arm around his neck. I had the front of his neck in the crook of my arm at the bend, like a sleeper hold. I pushed forward on the back of his head with my other hand as I squeezed with my inner arm tightening my grip, cutting off the blood and oxygen to his head. He was out in a matter of seconds. I let go a few seconds after he went limp because I didn't want him to die just yet. I put on some thick rubber gloves with a satisfying snapping sound; I wanted to play a bit first.

I looked around in a few of the drawers in his kitchen trying to find some kind of rope or duct tape or something to bind his hands and feet so he couldn't escape once he woke up. I eventually found some zip ties in the junk drawer which were even better. I found some duct tape in the cupboard and with that I taped his mouth shut so he wouldn't scream too loudly when he came to, and then I sat down in a chair in front of him waiting for him to wake up.

He was sitting there head lolling to the side in his chair, drooling through the side of his mouth under the tape. His head was slowly rocking in small circles as he started to come to. He still had crossed eyes; he was definitely higher than any one man ever ought to be. I looked around the room and spotted a backpack sitting on the floor. Inside of it was the package of all of the needles he was going to use to shoot speed into himself. There were about thirty of them counting the one he had just used, which was still sitting on the table in front of us, tainted with his junkie blood. One by one I began pulling them out of their packages and setting them on the table in front of me.

He was watching me with a confused look on his face. His look turned to one of terror though, as I grabbed small sections of his face between my thumb and forefinger and started to stick the needles through the flesh, one by one. His whimpers were quieted by the tape. I put about ten of them into his face. Two of them into each cheek, three across the forehead, and then decided to pierce three more down his neck. By the time I got to the bottom of his neck, he had stopped moving, in fear of more pain as I was not gentle with him. He just trembled now and his breathing had become faster through his nostrils.

By this point he had realized it wasn't just the drugs sending him on some sort of a bad high. His eyes had focused now and he appeared to have sobered up a bit. Probably all of the adrenaline coursing through his blood from my exactment of revenge for a woman I didn't even know. He tried pleading with me the best he could through the tape begging me to please stop. It was a bad move on his part because it just made me feel more sadistic and I wanted to push the limits of his pain tolerance. I might have felt bad if he hadn't done so many horrible things to a woman who put her heart and soul into him when she knew he wasn't worth any of it. In fact, she could have paid the ultimate price, all so he could get high.

I told him, "I have no sympathy for a woman beating, junkie piece of shit like you. Using someone's naive blind love for you to manipulate them into despicable things for your own gain? I only wish that I could drag this out for ever." I was disgusted with him.

He gave a rather impressive attempt at busting out of the zip ties. His face was turning so red I thought he might give himself an aneurism, which would have been an alternative way for Death to almost stop me a second time from killing him. When he could see he wasn't getting out of this situation by brute force, he looked at me and blinked motioning that he had something to say. I removed his tape with a fast rip, feeling giddy as his face grimaced in pain. Nothing he said would stop me from ending him but I was curious what he wanted to say. If he begged me to let him go, I was going to make it painful.

He started up instantly, "Look man, I know you want to hurt me, she must be your sister or something I get it man, I'm sorry I don't know what she told you but I didn't do it man, I didn't do nothing. Let me out of this chair man, I just want one more blast and you can do whatever you want, I promise." I thought I might not have heard him correctly at first, but I knew I understood him just fine. He actually wanted more drugs!

That did it. The rage consumed me beyond the boiling point and I started to take the needles thing to its extreme. I took another needle and shoved it straight through his cheek; I felt it stab into his tongue. I did the same thing to the other cheek and he started screaming. I was expecting that and was ready for it so as soon as he let out the beginnings of a yell I karate chopped the front of his throat with the side of my hand shutting his screaming off instantly. He looked surprised but made no more attempts to scream.

Not that anyone would hear him anyways, he didn't have very much power behind his voice, at least not right now as high as he was. He sat quietly besides the occasional whimper as I brought the needles to his face and pierced another spot, and another. There were only a handful of needles left now. The rest were stuck around his head and face making him look like the junkie version of Pinhead.

I wanted to see some real terror; I was surprised at how much I was enjoying this. I pointed one of the needles at his eyeball, allowing him to focus on it and see it coming slowly towards him. That set him off on a screaming tangent I couldn't stop him from attempting no matter how hard I hit him in the throat. He was screaming "HELP" for dear life and I actually got a bit concerned that someone may hear it.

Before I knew it, I had jammed a needle hard right into his voice box. He hadn't expected that one to happen and frankly, neither did I. The needle was blocking his voice box from being able to vibrate so he couldn't say anything anymore. I could still hear him breathing, it was a raspy phlegmy sound, but he couldn't make much more noise than that now. The only noises he made now were as he choked on the blood slowly gathering in his throat. I hoped I had blown his high now.

I grabbed one of the needles that was left and motioned slowly like I was going to stab him in his balls. His eyes widened and then, as if he could take no more, they rolled up into his head as he passed out. I didn't know how long the ex-girlfriend was going to be in the hospital or if she would come back here when she did, so I decided to go ahead and get this over with. I filled up the needle he had last used to shoot up with full of air and copied his procedure the best I could to pump his veins up. I tied the rubber band around his arm to let the blood gain some pressure and shot the entire plunger full of air into one of his pumped up veins.

Nothing was happening. He just breathed normally as he moaned trying to come to again. I untied his arm band frustrated that it didn't work. The effect was almost immediate, he began violently shaking, his skin turning a blue hue as his vein was clogged with an air bubble stopping the blood and oxygen from getting through. I realized that the arm band had been stopping the bubbles from going through; they had only been released when I let the pressure go back to normal. Then, he was dead.

I decided to let him be found. I left no fingerprints and any other evidence of me being here was nonexistent but I didn't want to leave him like this. If there were ghosts, I wanted him to be embarrassed as he was floating over his body when he was found. I carried him into the bedroom where I took his belt off of his pants, I then looped it around the bar in the closet and then around his neck so he was in a hanging position. I then pulled the front of his pants down so that his dick was hanging out and tucked his right hand into the elastic to hold it in place a little bit. It looked like he had stuck a bunch of needles into his face and neck and then came in here to choke himself and masturbate.

I knew that they would figure out the cause of death was the air bubble but the extra details would definitely confuse the hell out of the cops and make for a more likely unsolved homicide. I was sure they were going to write it off like my first murder feeling they had enough closure to shut the case down and sleep just fine at night. He was after all, just a junkie. I took one last look around making sure I hadn't forgotten anything that could lead back to me. I found nothing. I was proud of what I had accomplished. I was feeling so good by this time in fact that I felt it was time to pay a special someone a visit. First I needed to pay my visit to Curtis though, I had almost forgotten about him in all the excitement.

XVI

I went over to visit Curtis the next afternoon. There was no way I was going to make any kind of appearance though, without taking a long hot shower. I didn't feel guilty; I had only done what Karma should have done a long time ago. There was nothing inside me that screamed out in defense for the guy, even up to the bitter end he was pleading for his own life. Between some of his more coherent mumblings I could have sworn I heard him curse her even though she had done absolutely nothing to wrong him. He was just a true piece of shit and the world was now better off.

Curtis was glad to see me of course, shaking my hand warmly before leading the way to his gamer cave from the sweetest pits of hell. I already knew the drill, look and see what the newest games he had were and pick something out. I picked a free roam game so I didn't have to concentrate too much as my mind was bustling with last night's activities and wondering what was going to come of it. Curtis noticed right away that something was different with me.

"What's going on man? You seem down or something. Is everything alright?

"Oh me, yeah they're fine, I was just daydreaming about a girl." I said. That actually wasn't a lie either; I had been daydreaming about Lucas' mother quite a bit, mentally trying to prepare myself for that moment when I finally knocked on her door.

We heard his mother's voice coming from downstairs. "WHAT? You have got to be shitting me, when did this happen? Hold on, calm down, I can't understand you." Curtis and I inched towards the stairs where we could better hear what was going on since his mother's voice had taken on a more frantic tone now. "Okay honey calm down, I can't understand what you're saying." There was another pause as she listened to whoever was on the other end. Yeah, come by and see me, I'll see you when you get here." We heard her hang up the phone. She started laughing hysterically. Then we heard what sounded like sobs for a minute… then more laughing. We had no idea what was going on but I was pretty sure that she was on the phone with the meth heads ex-girlfriend.

Curtis asked me to wait for a minute and I nodded pretending to play the game. In reality I wasn't even paying attention. It didn't matter; Curtis was finding out what was going on with his mother so I would know soon enough I was sure. I began to have a miniature panic attack that hit me out of nowhere. I was having trouble breathing and my heart was racing, it felt too fast. I wasn't sure that I was up to meeting her as I had just murdered her boyfriend the night before. I didn't expect it all to hit me like this. I was going to have to make up some kind of excuse why I was going to have to leave.

Curtis came bounding up the stairs and into his room again just a little sooner than I would have liked as I was still feeling a bit dizzy. I wanted to know if I was right about her being the one who was coming over so I asked, "So what happened?"

I noticed Curtis looked a little bit pale. I don't think he noticed I wasn't feeling well as he looked at the ground while talking to me at first. "That was my dad I guess. That speed freak dude that I told you about last night was hanging dead in his closet. My dad took her over to the house to get her shit from him because she was planning on leaving him. I guess he left her first though." His eyes widened suddenly, "Oh my God! What if my dad did it!? My mom was all mad wanting him to; maybe that's why she was laughing so crazy. Shit dude… you picked a messed up day to come over."

I was speechless. Here his dad happened to be the one who found him after Curtis heard the argument between his mom and him. When Curtis father called it in he was walking out front and the guy's dealer happened to be walking up to the door just as he was walking out with the ex-girlfriend. He became suspect number one, but that lasted all of about ten minutes. He had about fifteen people that would vouch for him claiming that they were all at a party the night before with him. Whether it was true or not I don't know but he had so many people collaborate his story they had no choice but to keep looking.

I had taken off his zip ties after I killed him. They knew he was zip tied by the marks on his wrists and that he didn't stab himself in the throat, or pierce his own face because there were no fingerprints on any of the needles and there were no gloves in the house. Rule number one, don't leave behind evidence. So far they had no other suspects but Curtis would tell me later that his mother totally thought that his father had done it. His father of course was more than happy to claim it so long as it would keep his wife happy. He must have figured he would deal with the truth if the time ever came.

I knew that everything was going to be alright. I had gone over it with a clear head, I knew I had left nothing incriminating at the scene. It was just too easy to get away with murder when you picked the right person. This guy was refuse nobody cared about. He had nobody to claim the body besides his ex-girlfriend and she almost let him die a john doe. There wasn't much emotion when she looked down on him again though. Just a blank face and a single "Yep" and then she walked out looking lighter with every step that she was leaving behind involving him. I can't say I blamed her; he beat the shit out of her, and not just physically.

I decided to stay for a bit and calmed down steadily since I found out that it wasn't her coming over and was just his father. He was going to be so busy talking to Curtis mother that I doubted I would even see him before I left. I began to daydream about Lucas mother again once I calmed down and it had to be noticeable because Curtis started winning against me no matter what games we played and I was usually the winner every time even though they were his games.

"Hey I have to go somewhere brother, I'll have to stop by another time. It was great catching up, maybe next time there won't be so much drama." I smiled but he already knew I was kidding.

"Yeah, and maybe next time you won't be daydreaming about some girl the whole time so you'll be more fun to hang out with." He smiled back, a mutual understanding. I didn't say anything more, just gave him a quick fist bump before I turned around to walk out the door. My heart was beating faster than it had ever beaten before.

XVII

I knocked on the door with three solid knocks and waited what seemed to be the longest thirty seconds of my life. Finally I heard some noise and the door opened up to the gorgeous face of Lucas' mother standing before me. Well, usually she was gorgeous but right now she looked like she had been bawling her eyes out and drinking for days with no sleep. Her eyes were red and puffy, they were swollen and she had bags under them that showed she was more than a little bit exhausted. She probably hadn't slept well in months and I felt pangs of guilt for doing that to her. She stood there for a short time trying to figure out who I was and what I was doing there before finally speaking.

"I'm sorry; I wasn't expecting anyone to stop by." She wiped away some of her tears trying to regain her composure.

"I hope I'm not stopping by at a bad time, I was just in the neighborhood and I wanted to see how you were doing. I was a friend of Lucas from school." Again the feeling of guilt hit me for lying to her. I suddenly felt weird being here, she looked at me confused trying to remember if she had seen me before. She must have thought about it and felt it would be good to have company to talk with about her son. The guilt turned to relief as I saw her eyebrows relax from their upraised position. A small smile broke out on her lips bringing back a touch of that beautiful woman I knew she was.

"Well come on in, it's been a while since I have gotten the opportunity to talk with a friend of my sons." Her entire mood seemed to lighten now, she definitely had to have heard about me when we got into our fight and got suspended, but with her son being gone and her newly formed habit of drinking, she accepted my being a friend of Lucas with absolutely no further line of questioning to prove it. She was happy to see anyone from her son's life and as I stepped into the doorway, she even gave me a nice warm hug before letting me step inside the house. I felt her warm skin through her shirt and realized that she wasn't wearing a bra, I wondered if she was wearing panties.

"Please, have a seat." She told me as she motioned with her hand for me to sit down on the two cushioned thick comfy couch that was part of a new furniture set she had bought. No doubt she bought it to get rid of the old furniture that her husband liked to spend his life on. "Would you like something to drink?" She asked me.

"Thank you, that sounds great." I told her as she gave me a little smile and turned around to walk back towards the kitchen. It was amazing how much a simple thing as a smile could light up her entire face. What had a minute ago seemed like an aged depressed face had suddenly lost ten years and seemed to be losing more by the minute. I knew that she didn't go anywhere anymore; she had quit her job and become a hermit.

I had snuck by a few times to see her and had been lucky to catch her on a couple of nights when she was in a better mood. One night in particular I found her masturbating and I finished myself off with her underneath the window. Any other time she would be crying and cursing her husband for being the alcoholic killer she would always remember him as. I could hear her shuffling around and I heard the water being turned on, I realized that she had gone in to compose herself, maybe splash a little cold water on her face.

After about five minutes she came back out looking miraculous. She had dressed in a simple pair of blue sweat bottoms that had "juicy" written across her ass, and a light blue t shirt. She had done something to her face that made the puffiness invisible and had pulled her hair up into a scrunchie letting her face be seen in full. I almost couldn't stop looking at her.

She came back in and handed me a cold can of Cola. She had gotten herself another beer, which didn't surprise me but I said nothing. "It's hard losing a son to a psychotic husband." she told me as she took a long drink of her beer.

"I think you deserved much better than someone like that. I can't believe he went so far!" I could see her eyes narrow as he was mentioned but she agreed with a nod and drank the rest of her beer down, going back into the kitchen to get another one she downed almost just as fast. Her trips to the kitchen were finally slowing down after 5 beers that I had counted. She didn't talk very much at first; I wasn't sure what to tell her about Lucas, I just recanted things I had seen him do before when I was trying not to be noticed by him. There were times he might smile at girls, or other times when people might laugh about things that he said. I tried to stay on the friend side of stories. Mentioning things about him that seemed to impress the friends he hung out with. I talked about how he was good at sports, and had a charisma that people seemed to like even though to me in reality, he was just an asshole. I didn't tell her that of course. I mentioned anything I could remember about him that could make her smile. She began laughing after a while, remembering her son and listening to me tell her the memories I could pull out of my ass. Then out of nowhere she began to cry.

"This is all my fault." She sobbed between deep breaths and embarrassed looks my way. "Lucas only died because I refused to do what I should have done a long time ago and left his father's ass. I don't even know what kept me with him for so long, he didn't do anything but speak hypocrisies and beat us both whenever he was in a bad mood, which was all the time!"

"Hey, hey," I tell her, reaching over giving her a hug, which she sunk right into. "None of that was ever your fault," I rubbed her back lightly while keeping her in a tight embrace. Her body softened in my arms. I could tell she needed this kind of attention and I was growing more excited by the second. I had gotten into significant shape since her son was alive; I liked to keep my body as fit as I could now so that I never have to go through a situation like tripping over something while trying to kill someone. Next time something like that happened I might not be so lucky.

She was so tired of being here alone and having nobody around. All of her friends had quit talking to her long ago because she fought with them over her drunken husband and they moved on. She also didn't have parents that were close to her. She was truly all by herself. She started to pull away a bit and I hugged her a little tighter taking a chance and letting my lust take over hoping she felt the energy and responded to it. She started lightly shivering and moved her face up to look into my eyes. I took the opportunity and moved in fast to kiss her softly on the lips.

She stared blankly at me for a few seconds having what must have been a good fight in her mind. Then she began pulling my head to hers and French kissing me hungrily. I kissed back just as passionately; I had wanted this for a long time. I was rubbing her shoulders and moving my hands lightly down her arms making my way toward her breasts. She let it happen, I figured the alcohol was doing its part to help me accomplish this so easily but I didn't care. It was like a dream come true and I didn't ever want to wake up. I squeezed her ample breasts lightly amazed at how solid they felt getting much more than a handful, they were just as perfect as I had always imagined.

A light moan escaped her lips as she kissed me, growing more passionate by the second. I knew that this was no ordinary make out session, this was heading only one place, and it was a place I wanted to be more than anything else. I could resist no longer, I moved my left hand softly down the side of her face, softly touching her face under her chin, as I moved my right hand down to her thighs. Her sweats were elastic and I easily slid my hand inside them confirming officially that she was indeed not wearing panties.

I let my fingers explore and felt her moistened and warm pussy lips, she was soaked already. I couldn't help it, I started shaking. I wasn't sure why, it wasn't cold inside but I couldn't stop it. I was so excited. She seemed to like that because she smiled and started rubbing my crotch. I was already hard being so excited and she unbuttoned the front of my pants pulling out my cock and licking her lips before she started sucking on it.

She was moaning as she sucked on me as if I was the most delicious thing she had ever tasted. I felt myself about to explode already as she sucked and she pulled me closer grabbing my ass and shoving me deeper in her throat than I had even been inside of my own hand before. I couldn't help it, knowing she wanted it so bad I pumped the biggest load I had ever shot out of me, inside her mouth. She stroked it slowly clamping around my dick with her lips and tongue milking every drop into her throat. She swallowed it all down and used her hands to help ease it all out. She softly sucked on me for another minute like my dick was a cream filled popsicle trying to get every drop down. I was still rock hard, so she turned around and pulled her pants down just below her ass, offering her most intimate parts to me.

She was so wet that I slid right inside; I slid in so fast in fact that I almost lost my balance. This was everything I had imagined it being, I wanted to stay here forever inside of her. I was surprised at how well she hugged my dick, I didn't figure on her being so tight but that proved me wrong with every stroke. We didn't even have to leave the bed; I had never been more comfortable or felt so right. The circumstances could have been better but besides that this was my new heaven. I started thrusting as deep as I could inside of her giving her every inch that I had to give as powerfully as my hips would allow. "That feels so good, I'm going to cum." She said, in such an erotic way that I felt myself starting to get that feeling like I was going to cum again. I could feel her pussy contracting around me and I couldn't help but let my 2nd load go, this time inside her. I could feel her cum as she got much wetter. I let her throbbing subside while stroking with nice deep pumps both of us using each other to milk the other completely. She started to moan again and I knew she was going to cum once more. When she was done and I was emptied I was still pretty hard so I figured I would try some dirty talk. She kept rocking back into me and I knew I could keep going for her.

"Yeah baby, fuck that pain away."

I instantly wished I hadn't said that. The entire mood changed with those words as she backed off of me, easing my dick out of her. She sat there for a minute in awkward silence suddenly looking horrified. The look on her face said that I had just reminded her of what was really going on, and she was ashamed. I watched her face turn down, and the color in her face first flushed and then paled, as she ran through what was happening in her mind. "What have I done?" She asked. I didn't think she was actually asking me but rather talking out loud so I said nothing. I could see the shame on her face as she apologized profusely over and over again saying: "I'm sorry, I'm so sorry." She began crying again. "What kind of a cougar am I?" I could hear her asking between her sobs. I'm no better than a drunken pedophile!

"I'm old enough to have wanted this myself!" I tried to reassure her, but I had no argument that she would listen to. It had been a while since Lucas had died but to her he was still 16. In her mind I was suddenly a child and she was upset with herself. I was more upset at myself for saying something so stupid at such a horrible time.

"I think that I need you to go… please." She said to me with a tone in her voice that said there would be no changing her mind. I was feeling more awkward by the second so I reluctantly agreed with her. Her eyes had gone empty, maybe it would be better if I left now and gave her time to calm down. I suddenly felt like I had ruined her entire life and the sad truth was that I had. I got up and got dressed having a hard time looking at her because it just made me sad all over again. I went over to where she was sitting facing the other way and tried to give her a hug and a kiss goodbye.

She didn't even look at me, just sat there, I gave her a light kiss on the corner of her mouth but she didn't react besides her lip quivering as she tried not to cry. She tensed as I hugged her making me feel like I had just raped her or something and I felt that leaving without another word was probably going to be the best course of action. I had no idea what to say to her, I felt my face growing hot and I knew that I was turning red; luckily she wasn't looking at me.

I closed the door behind me only looking back for a second; she was walking the other way towards her room at the back of the house. I went around the back of the house so I could walk back home through the woods that connected to my property where I could be alone. I was still a bit confused about what the hell had just happened, it was like the best dream and a nightmare both rolled into one experience. How could something that was going so perfect, turn sour like that so incredibly fast? How could it get any worse? I was lost in the middle of that thought when suddenly I heard a gunshot behind me. Her window was open and it was loud and clear. I felt my shoulders go up towards the top of my head as I involuntarily jumped.

My eyes filled with tears right away and they didn't stop even when I felt like I wasn't going to be able to breathe anymore. I fell to my knees and cried harder than I had ever cried in my entire life. I swore I was going to die from a broken heart. When I finally could breathe again I fought gravity the best I could and got to my shaky knees. By the time I got home I could hear the sirens echoing through the trees on their way to her house. Someone must have heard the gun go off and called them. I already knew she wasn't going to make it, she had no fight left. I had killed my first and only love, which would haunt me for the rest of my life. I wished I could take that stupid sentence back. If only…

XVIII.

I lost a lot of my passion for life the night she died. I felt completely disappointed in myself for being the tool that convinced her to pull the trigger. I know I hadn't done anything physically to harm her but I might as well have put the gun in her hand for her. I was glad that I had graduated already because I couldn't have handled school right now if I tried.

I didn't go anywhere, my mother had no idea what was wrong with me and I wasn't in any sort of mood to talk about it. I just had to give myself time to get over it, I needed to grieve. I couldn't get it out of my mind how she thought of herself as a pedophile. I had a sudden intensified hatred for them that seemed to go beyond rational. I wanted to mutilate one. The thought consumed me now and the only thing that would settle me I already knew was going to be doing just that.

I was walking down the street a short time later when I saw a weird looking guy sitting on a park bench that caught my eye who was staring at these little kids playing on the playground. None of the kids were looking at him like they were at the other adults that were there. He was dressed in a red hoodie with the newest hot band staring off of his chest like they were trying to seduce whoever was on the other side. Obviously a band he was a little too old for but it sure would give him a reason to strike up conversations with young people who weren't. He looked like a promising prospect; I had a feeling I had manifested just the person I needed as if by magic. I walked over and sat down by him. He had thick horn rimmed glasses that accentuated his dark concentrated eyes.

He didn't even notice me sitting next to him until I spoke. "Which ones yours?" I already knew the answer.

He seemed surprised he hadn't noticed me; he said "Oh, I don't have any kids. I was walking around and wanted to rest my feet for a few and saw this bench." He gave me a smile someone might give a camera when they weren't in the mood to be photographed. I felt suddenly disgusted when I saw him smile; his teeth were crooked and looked as if they hadn't been brushed in quite a while, adding to his already repulsive look. I wanted to punch him in the face just then, but I kept my cool. I wanted to get him to open up so I could find out if he was what I was looking for. I had to play this one carefully.

"Kids are so lucky, they're so innocent and oblivious to the fact that life is going to get fucked up, you know?" I said.

He was watching one little girl more intently than the others as he spoke. "Yeah, one day they'll grow up and use and abuse each other. The world can be a dark place." I thought that was a weird thing to say but went with it, seeing how far he would go with this.

"Especially one like that." I said, pointing towards the girl he seemed to be so entranced by. She was probably about 8 or so. She had her hair to the side in a ponytail and was climbing the slide trying to race her friend to the top who was using the stairs. "She's gonna be a little heartbreaker someday." He looked around nervously making me wonder if I had taken it too far with that one. To my relief, he quietly agreed. We talked more after that, he warmed up quickly about his darker desires and pointed out one kid in particular he liked much sooner than I expected him to. It was a little boy of about 10 years of age. I was feeling more confident now. I decided to go for it, "I have a couple of young boys like that where I stay that keep their mouths shut. If the price is right I might invite you over, maybe let you meet one. Its rare meeting other people into this kind of thing, it would be nice to share it sometime."

He breathed a sigh of relief. "I live with my parents so that's great that you can host. They might think it was weird if I had some strange guy and some young boys over." I had the feeling they knew about his little secret. I gave him the address to the junkie's old place. I figured it was a safe place as it was abandoned due to him being brutally murdered in it and no killer having been found. I already knew that nobody came around much and it was dark and secluded enough that noise wouldn't be an issue unless someone were right outside. Luckily people are afraid of ghosts and avoided that place like the plague.

I said, "Show up tonight around 7 and I'll have the kids over for a sleepover. Bring some Funyuns and condoms because I like to be safe with my little toys. Also bring some kind of good liquor because they loosen up and get much friskier when they're buzzed." I watched a smile forming across his face getting bigger and bigger, especially when I mentioned the liquor loosening them up. I said my goodbyes and left. *I was going to enjoy killing him*. I thought to myself as I walked away leaving him sitting there watching the little kids on his bench.

That night I waited across from the junkie's old house for the sick fuck to show up. Finally, around 7 p.m. I saw him walking up towards the house. He looked nervous. He probably expected 'To Catch a Predator' to be there. I almost wished they were here, just to see him embarrassed on national TV. He had walked up from a block away in case he had to run and get to his car. He had a small brown paper bag with him and I felt a little more hate for him that he actually brought the liquor. I thought about the last time I saw her and how she was getting drunk and had called herself a pedophile. I wanted to hurt this guy so bad. It was almost too much to bear; I needed to get to it.

I snuck up on him scaring the shit out of him for a second. He hadn't seen or heard me come up. "Hey man," I told him, "I was beginning to think you weren't coming." I could see he was still nervous and I pointed to the brown bag "Is that the liquor?" He showed me inside the bag was a 750ml bottle of 100 proof root beer tasting liquor. The sicko had even gotten candy tasting liquor that kids might enjoy. "Cool man, hey wait here a minute I'll be right back." I went around to the backside of the house to go through a broken window and unlock the door. There weren't any close neighbors around so nobody saw him or I standing in the yard. I walked through the house and opened the front door letting him in. It was all dark inside and I could see it made him uneasy. He looked around the empty house the best he could in the darkness and I walked behind him leading him into the kitchen.

"House seems kind of empty, where is everything?" he asked. I didn't answer right away. Instead, I grabbed the liquor from him and opened it taking a nice long shot. It was like liquid fire, but delicious and did indeed taste a lot like root beer. I take one more large pull off of the bottle taking a second more to savor the flavor of that last drink as I felt the hot liquid move down my body, warming me up.

"I love when sicko's bring me liquor," I say. A confused look spread over his face and he attempted to run back outside but I had blocked him in the kitchen. I punched as hard as I could directly into the middle of his face, knocking him down like dead weight. I watched him for a minute as he tried to gather his senses. He looked up at me stunned with wild eyes. He was bleeding from the lip. "You know right here in this very kitchen the world lost another sick fuck like you" I cracked my knuckles one hand after the other.

"Where's the kids man?" he asked. I was aghast, he reminded me of the meth head asking for just "One more hit."

"There are no kids, you fuck. Even after all this you still thought I was for real?"

He scrambled for something to say, his eyes darting back and forth rapidly as he thought. "I'm a cop; I have people outside." He said, "You better let me go so I can tell them there are no kids in here."

"I don't think so," I said. "I've been watching the house since before you arrived first of all and second, the cops would have been here waiting for a child molester, not sending someone in with condoms and liquor to come and see the kids." He looked panicked not knowing quite what to expect. I was sure he thought I was going to turn him in, but there would be no such luck for him. I started to kick him, he tried to block the flurry of kicks but I kept aiming for spots he wasn't protected against. He couldn't keep up and was getting pretty beaten.

When he couldn't block anymore I got a couple of satisfying kicks to his unprotected face and then picked him up off of the floor. I wanted to take the fight or flight right out of him and now it was done. I dragged him into the corner of the kitchen and zip tied him over a milk crate I found in the corner earlier that was screwed into the floor. I wasn't sure but figured the meth head was high one time and screwed it into the floor as a seat for someone to sit on.

His hands and feet were bound down near the floor, he wasn't going anywhere. Once he was nice and secured, I gagged him by stuffing a rag in his mouth and cut off his clothing taking special care to make sure I cut him a little as I went along. I wanted him to suffer as my heart suffered when my dead queen called herself a sick fuck like this piece of shit. I was going to make him suffer more than anybody should. He managed to spit out the rag and began screaming. I did what I did to the junkie before, hit him in his throat

"You like to fuck kids?" I asked as I grabbed the condoms out of the bag he had brought in. I took another pull off of the root beer liquor. I was feeling much better now. "Yeah you're a cop alright." I said as I waved the condom box in the air in front of his face. He looked down in defeat knowing his lies wouldn't work anymore. I dumped the bag with the condoms on the floor in front of him. to my delight a pre rolled joint fell out as well, I lit it and began to smoke it. I was going to need to remain calm and not get too emotional. "Relax," I said, "I'm not going to fuck you in the ass, I'm not gay." He seemed less tense after that but his eyes widened as he watched me grab a broom from the side of the refrigerator that had been left here.

He was gagged again so his scream came out sounding more like "MMMMM!" rather than "No!" I unrolled a condom I had taken out of the pack and slipped it over the end of the broom until it was fully unrolled. I had to wonder to myself who had a dick this big? It was a good foot in length down the end of the broom, much more than the average man needed. I could hear him moaning what I'm sure was the word "Please" over and over again. That just made me more focused on my goal here. I stuck the condom covered broom inside his asshole and I started pushing it in and out of him, pleased at how uncomfortable this was making him. He began crying, humiliated as he wanted to make a child feel tonight. As I fucked him with the broom, I started slapping the back of his head demoralizing him even further.

He screamed with pain as I yelled at him, "How's it feel to have things done you know are wrong to you?" I could feel my face growing redder by the second as my anger began taking over.

I could hear him through his gagged screams trying to say "sorry, I'm sorry." I left the broom in his ass, a good ten inches deep and walked around to look him in his eyes.

"I think you used your libido for all the wrong reasons," I told him. He looked confused and upset. This wasn't what he had in mind. He might have had a worry about jail but being bent over in an abandoned house and violated by a broom was probably the furthest thing from his mind. He had no idea where this might go, but he was starting to see a larger picture unfold. I walked around behind him and slapped his ass telling him, "This ride is about to get serious." He screamed once more as I shoved the broom with a fair amount of strength, deep into his rectum.

Everything in him froze, including his breathing. His eyes were as wide as they could get. His skin turned as pale as albino skin and blood started pouring out of his ass. I had pierced something inside of him. He started to cry through the gag now uncontrollably. He sounded like a scared 6 year old kid which sent me into a rage since I was sure he had made little kids cry in pain and fear like he was now. Before I could stop myself I started kicking the brooms sweeper end, each time nailing the broom deeper into his body. I felt a rage like he had killed my love himself coming over me and I kicked harder and harder until finally I could see the brooms handle end pushing against the skin inside of his shoulder on the left side of his body. I pushed on the bristled end and I could see the broom moving under the skin of his shoulder.

I laughed for a second but then it seemed like I could almost feel the pain from this and reflex took over. I felt sick suddenly and had to run into the bathroom to throw up. I made sure to flush and went back out to the kitchen. I grabbed his wallet from his back pocket and found his ID with his address. I wanted to send his hands and balls to his parents. He said he lived with them I just hoped that this was the right address. He had a shocked look on his dead face and something snapped in my brain, I recognized him from a dream I'd had as a kid where I was cutting him up in the tub. I had also seen this face one time in a dream where I opened the refrigerator, only he had no eyes. I got a sudden feeling of déjà vu and I walked back into the bathroom. I started to laugh. The tub in this house was the same as the one in my dream. My stomach growled again, I was feeling hungry now.

And they try to say destiny has no place in life.

XIX.

Life spiraled into a whirlwind of blood and last breaths for a while after that. My resolve had become rigid. I had finally accepted the new me and I was no longer as specific about my victims. I was becoming less of a vigilante, and more of a stone cold killer. I no longer killed for the right reasons. Something in me snapped when she died. Not long after that happened, my mother moved out, leaving me the house. We didn't speak often anymore, I had become… consumed.

I lost a part of myself and no longer trusted that my needs wouldn't hurt those that I loved. It was probably good that she moved, I had to cut my feelings away from it all, I couldn't become so broken over the way things unfold. I had gone from killing people who I thought deserved it, to just anybody I found I decided to kill, if nothing more than to fill up my freezer. I still tried to go after people that were wastes of life but occasionally the thought crossed my mind that maybe I was just deluded to think anybody at all deserved it. Lucas was an asshole, but he was just a kid now that I looked back at it. Though I must admit at the time, I didn't really care.

My newfound nonchalance led me to start killing random people who just happened to be in the wrong place at the wrong time. I even went so far as to snag a drunk woman at an ATM machine one night. I was a little bit drunk that night and decided to go grocery shopping. It was my idea at the time of an inside joke. I had the sense of mind luckily to carry a black ski mask with me in case anything were to come up where I would need to protect my identity.

She became my meat for the month after I took her body through the process of making her into meal sized steaks. I had the nagging thought that she didn't deserve to die like all the others had but I quickly pushed it out of my head every time it came up until it was no longer in the forefront. It was always in the back of my mind though, it just became easier to ignore.

I began going to the big city and parking close to the city park where I knew some of the homeless people slept. The first time I went there was at 3 a.m. and I only saw one of them, an older man who was asleep at the request of the bottle he had been drinking. He lay there with a half-smile probably dreaming about being in a warm bed and cuddling his sweetie, which was how he was cuddling his half full bottle. I stomped on his neck so fast and hard that he most likely didn't feel a thing. I had to carry him back to my car and take him home to chop his body up. The whole thing was fast and pretty quiet. It was also so late that I doubted anyone was awake who had seen or heard it.

One stomp ended this man's miserable existence… and further damned mine. I tried not to let it bother me and I wound up killing a couple more homeless men a few months after that night each in a similar and swift manner.

It's unknown why but after a while every killer eventually turns to the prostitutes as a safe target to murder. I found a particularly cute girl one night named Trina standing on a corner looking for a date. She was wearing a short black leather miniskirt with white and black leggings that accentuated her wild side in compliment with her wild hair that was in puffy blond locks flowing down her head on all sides. She wore it like a girl from the 70's might have worn. I asked her to rent a room for the night in a quiet dark little motel a bit back from the road off of the highway. She seemed a bit uneasy at first. "Why you need me to do it? You can't get a room in your own name or what?"

I replied smoothly, "I just want to fuck; I don't want to be arrested. I have a warrant out for prostitution already and they're watching the hotels for my name to pop up."

She seemed satisfied with that answer and visually relaxed, her shoulders becoming less rigid. "Oh I understand that honey, let me tell you I get harassed by the cops all the time in my profession. Well as long as it's your money paying for it I'm cool with that I guess." she went inside to rent the room. She came back out after about five minutes and led me to the room across the way, number 13 on the first level. "So what you want me to do baby?" She asked once we were inside.

"I want you to be my forbidden love thing. I want you to give yourself to me against your better judgment… and remember, be passionate." She looked at me weird, she must not be so used to specifics like this, but she agreed. After all, she was a professional.

Nothing about it was the same; this hooker could never hope to be her. She wasn't nearly as passionate for one thing, she may not have been made for acting but she was most definitely built for fucking. All that didn't matter though. She was full of one liner's you would expect a hooker to say like: "Fuck me daddy!" and then there was the "Oh my god, you're so big!" it felt scripted and I'm sure it was. She kept saying things like she loved me and acted like our meeting was an everyday thing instead of a fantasy coming true. I tried to accept that it wouldn't be the same as with my love but it was more than that. I felt more like I was fucking a hooker than living my fantasy again. It was awkward, from the moment we sat down, until the moment I found my hands wrapped around her neck.

Her face turned a much darker color than it had been before and was now wearing a look of panic. I could see her tongue flicking in and out of her mouth as she tried to breathe, but instead of trying to fight me off or scratch me or something to free herself; she was merely trying to pry my hands off of her neck. It wasn't going to happen, I knew that it was too late to let go now. I had turned a corner I couldn't come back from. It just felt wrong. Lucas' mother wasn't in love with me, it was a passion thing and it was a thing that eased pain for her at least for a brief moment.

Then this hooker Trina started telling me I was her dream man as she kissed me like I was her long lost love or something. She was probably thinking that was what I wanted to hear, but it wasn't. My love was a forbidden fruit. It wasn't meant to happen, that's why I believe it went so wrong like it did. Now this hooker was trying to gasp for air but it was too late. I had to squeeze harder.

I heard her neck bone snap, her eyes went a little wider and I released my grip. Her body slumped to the floor, her eyes oddly calm, as if right before she died something told her she was going to be alright. I watched them go from panic to relaxed which could have been the lack of blood but it didn't matter, I had already strangled her to death.

Her blond curly hair was splayed out around her head silhouetting her expression like she was a model in a photo shoot. Her half naked tight body lay on the floor as if she were posing for a lingerie magazine for the dead. Her black leggings were held up by straps running down the side of her legs which were a little bent at the knees-one atop the other and she wore a small thin strapped white shirt. Her pink panties hugged her firm ass showing off the curvature of her hips and for one brief moment, she was the most beautiful picture I could ever hope to see. It almost made me want to fuck her. What was I thinking? I couldn't have sex with a dead body, could I? Had I lost my mind? Not this time, I wanted another living, breathing, passionate girl, so I could try and relive my time with... her again.

I decided to find myself another hooker. I would have to get two of them this time, just in case. I needed to watch my emotions this time around. I didn't have time to dispose of all kinds of bodies to cover up my lack of control developing recently. I was already going to have to chop Trina's body up and eat her; I couldn't be leaving trails of bodies all over the place. I had eaten the homeless people and a few random strangers over these last several years.

I was in my 30's now and was in a regular routine of killing and eating people. It was starting to feel more now that it was a necessity rather than an enjoyment for me. It felt like I was on the wrong path at times and I was losing the passion for it anymore but kept doing it. Similar to a junkie who loses the love for shooting up but keeps doing it because it's become a habit. I think I was just getting more addicted to murder and eating human flesh.

I was reminded of a man I had heard about a few years back named Issei Sagawa. Issei had been taking some classes at the Sorbonne and had invited a fellow classmate named Renee Hartevelt to his apartment to talk about literature, or so he said. When she got there Sagawa went behind her and shot her in the back of the neck at the table and then had sex with her corpse. He started nibbling on her nose and part of one of her breasts. According to him, "It had no smell or taste and melted in my mouth like raw tuna," That's what he wrote in 'In the Fog', his bestselling cannibalism encounter with Renee. "Finally, I was eating a beautiful white woman and thought nothing was so delicious!" By the time he was done he had eaten most of her leg as well. The thought that someone could be so cruel to someone innocent occurred to me and I looked at it with distaste at one time. Yet here I had done the same thing multiple times, except I never ate raw human. That was still pretty gross to me.

Also, I doubt I would get as lucky as Issei if I was ever caught. In custody Sagawa was found incompetent to stand trial and put into the Paul Giraud mental asylum in Paris. Through his powerful family connections he was transferred to a hospital in Tokyo. Within 15 months of hospitalization his influential father somehow managed to get him released. By then, Sagawa had become a national celebrity, an accomplished author and his story was told in the song "Too Much Blood" by the Rolling Stones.

At least he had good taste in food. Humans were a rather delectable dish now that I had become accustomed to them. For the most part they are very tasty and soft, like a soft fish if it's cooked right and other times more like chicken and yet others where it would turn out like pork chops. It depended on how they were cooked and what kind of crap they ate usually. Compare it to the difference between chicken grown with steroids and chicken grown without. The meat will stay juicier the fresher it is. Lately though, everyone seemed to be a little dry.

I had been seeing the faces of the people I had eaten the flesh from in my mind. It was enough to ruin my appetite a couple of times. At least when I killed someone that I thought deserved it I could spitefully chew on them as a sort of revenge. When they had done nothing however and I killed them, it was a lot harder to stomach when those thoughts came forward.

I decided tonight wasn't the night to figure this morality of my killings thing out, I still wanted to fulfill my fantasy brewing around in my head. So I hid Trina's dead body in my motel room's bathtub. Her body slumped down, her arms and legs sprawled out like a ragdoll with that empty stare looking at the ceiling as if something crazy just happened up there. I went back out into the night on the prowl.

Before long, I found a couple of girls that looked ripe for the picking. A short haired cute redhead named Candy and a long haired brunette with purple contacts that called herself Violet. They were both wearing pretty much the same thing, next to nothing. It was warm out tonight, they were wearing thigh high see through nightgowns you could see their black underwear under. They reminded me of the girls you might see on the back of a porno movie. I pulled up and asked them if they would like to be mine for the night. Both of them walked over to me bending down giving me a good shot of their cleavage as they leaned in the window. "That depends how much you wanna spend big boy," short haired Candy said with a seductive smile.

"How much for the night… for the both of you?" I asked reaching into my pocket.

"$1000 for 4 hours" she said, "for both of us." I agreed and showed them a wad of cash. They both smiled and the brunette Violet shot a glance toward a red Lumina that was parked in the shadows at the corner of the alleyway. She raised her hand as if to say bye and then they got in my car.

XX.

I drove them back to my motel room which Trina had so graciously gotten for me for the night and took them inside. I was so busy checking them out that I hardly remembered the drive to the motel. They were touching each other sensuously as if they had been together all along and it was very distracting. It was probably a good thing not many people were out driving tonight because I might have hit one of them had there been. As soon as we got inside I told them to take their nightgowns off. They both did as I asked and revealed to me some very nice bodies. Violet had a couple of scars on her stomach that I guessed were C-sections from unplanned babies but they were hardly noticeable. They were both gorgeous.

I told them to start kissing each other as I walked behind them and took off their bras, one at a time. Making sure to spend a little time holding and feeling the fullness of their breasts, admiring how perky they were. I told them to rub their tits together while they were kissing. I walked behind Violet and put my arms behind her joining in on the closeness. Candy was eyeing me while she kissed Violet and I felt the tingle starting in my crotch. I walked to the side of them and leaned Violet down so she could lay back on the bed.

I went behind Candy and wrapped one hand around her throat and with the other pulled her skimpy panties down to her knees. She took my lead and leaned forward on the bed still kissing Violet. She offered up her ass for me and I started rubbing it with my hands. It was quite nice. She wasn't quite wet yet but was moist and a little sticky. I could smell more than just an excited woman. There was a distinct smell of mixed sex permeating the air now. I smacked her ass and rubbed her with my other hand as they kissed each other.

Violet started lifting her ass and touching Candy's leg, starting to get turned on. Candy responded by touching violet back, rubbing her as she rolled her hips slowly in a mesmerizing circle. I was now standing naked behind Candy growing more with every little moan they were putting out. I wanted to see just how passionate they would get.

"Violet I want you to lick Candy's pussy nice and clean." I pushed Candy forward so she could get her tongue bath. Violet shot me a defiant glare for a second obviously aware of what kind of mess that might be but she must have been trained well to feel the customer was always right because it only lasted a second before she did what I wanted. She was cleaning Candy up real nice; I liked what I was seeing. She got deep in her with her tongue and was making her dripping wet. While Candy was moaning I crawled on the bed in front of her so she could take my now fully erect member into her mouth. "Make it nice and wet for me." I said.

She smiled and moved forward not saying a word but taking me into her mouth like it was her favorite pastime. It probably helped that she was also getting her pussy eaten at the same time, nevertheless she was on it. I tried to imagine it was Lucas' mom while she sucked me. She definitely knew what she was doing but the passion just wasn't the same. Candy knew how to suck like a master, I'm sure from all the practice she had obviously gotten but she kept stopping right when I felt the zone coming on and moaning from Violet eating all the cum out of her.

It was definitely distracting me from maintaining the memory I was trying to fuck to. I pulled my dick out of her mouth and went back around behind her. I wanted her to clean Violet up for me now so I told her to pull her panties down while I took her from behind. She was very wet now and had gotten her pussy cleaned up fairly well by Violet's tongue. I tried to get the feeling back as I thrust myself deep into her. She had a surprisingly tight hole for someone in her profession I thought but nothing about this was bringing the feelings I wanted. She pushed backwards onto me nice and hard every time I thrust into her but it wasn't quite on time like Lucas' mother had been. She was just a bit off because she was trying to get herself off too and Lucas' mom had no problems with that, she got off over and over again with ease.

I remembered standing under her window and watching her rub lotion on herself and thought about how hard I had cum that first time when I was so young. Candy noticed that I got harder and gasped, pausing her tongue lashing to look back at me while biting her lip. I pushed once more nice and strong deep into her before I pulled out all the way. I whispered to her, "I want to fuck you in the shower." I looked at Violet who was waiting for further directions. "Wait out here for a bit, I'll come play more with you soon."

Violet rolled her eyes but must not have cared too much because she just said, "Fine." and grabbed the remote to turn on the TV.

I walked Candy into the bathroom, careful not to turn on the light so she wouldn't look in the tub. When she was all the way in and the door was shut, I held her from behind like I was going to hug her and with my arm around her shoulder. I moved slowly until her neck was in the fold of my elbow and then I tightened my arm as I pushed on the back of her head until she passed out. It only took 10 seconds before she lost consciousness. Since that move cuts off the blood to the head, she didn't even realize what was happening until it was too late, she just gasped and tried grabbing my arms to unlock my grip but a few seconds later and it was too late.

Her arms flailed randomly and then she went limp. I quickly turned the light on and tied her by the hands up to the showerhead over Trina's body. I grabbed the hunting knife I brought in earlier to cut up Trina and went back to the tub. She started to wake up since I hadn't choked her long enough to kill her but I jammed my knife deep into the side of her throat, slicing a trench like gash into her neck and sawing out the front. She woke up instantly but didn't scream or do much besides open her eyes wide and then shut them again.

I rubbed the blood on her face feeling how slick it was and then felt myself get rock hard as her wound pumped the blood out. I wanted to fuck her with her own blood at that moment. I was altogether disgusted and turned on at the same time, probably a result of not getting off for so long. I stood up next to her and put my dick inside of her using the blood dripping down her body as a hot lube. It was warm and comfortable just like I had imagined it would be… at least at first.

I started thrusting hard now trying to finish but after a couple of minutes I realized that I couldn't. Something about this was all wrong. The blood didn't stay slick like I imagined it would, it became sticky too fast and pretty soon I was distracted thinking about how the blood might dry while I was fucking her and start cutting me. I wondered how long it would be until she started feeling cold to me. It wasn't long after that I went limp.

My eyes started to fill with tears. What the fuck was I doing? My obsession was spinning out of control and I felt powerless to stop it. I now had a hooker out there I had to kill that was watching TV waiting for us, as well as the two in here that were dead. What the fuck was I going to do? I turned on the shower so I could wash the blood off of my body and get a hold of my panic, careful not to lose my balance between the two dead bodies. I knew I would just have to take one again after cutting them up but it made me feel better anyways.

The water was hot and felt refreshing. It was spraying through the circle of Candy's arms as her lifeless body hung from the showerhead. Her face was relaxed but her eyes were closed so it wasn't as weird as it could have been. Most of her blood had drained out of her and was down the drain now but she would still have plenty left when I cut her up. For now I just laid her on top of Trina.

I needed to get back out there with Violet now; I had been in here almost a half hour already! I wondered if she was even out there still. I opened the door slowly and walked out of the bathroom. I saw her heels hanging off the bed and thought she might have fallen asleep. I could hear the television on a commercial about a used auto dealer as I walked around the corner. When I looked at Violet, I didn't know what the hell to do.

She was dead. Apparently she didn't like rejection and had shot up some from the looks of it, bad heroin. She had foam around her mouth and her veins were pumped out of her neck from the stress of having a seizure or something I guessed. At least I wouldn't have to kill her now.

I breathed a small sigh of relief. I looked down and noticed that she had tried ruffling through my pants. She also had her nightgown and underwear back on. I'm sure was planning on robbing and leaving me seconds after I went inside the bathroom with Candy. I wasn't stupid though, I never would have left my wallet in the pants with her out there and me in the bathroom. I locked my wallet and money in the glove box of my car while they both got out posing their asses in ways I couldn't wait to try stuffing. She hadn't thought about that as my keys were still in the left pocket of my jeans. She must have given up and decided to just get high and wait instead.

I walked back into the bathroom and surveyed the scene. I had Candy with a hole in her neck, a bloody hand smear down her face. She wouldn't be quite as messy now since I had drained a lot of her blood. Some of Candy's blood had leaked out of her neck onto the floor but not very much. Only about a six inch circle on the floor was all. I didn't think I had room for all these bodies in my freezer no matter how small I was going to cut them up. I figured I could dismember Candy first since she was already started; technically I hadn't killed Violet so I figured I would just let her be found.

The room was in Trina's name anyways and there were no ties to me here. It would be a short investigation if I cleaned up well enough. They usually didn't put up too much of a fight over hookers. The question of the blood is just visual, meaning what people don't see they usually don't question. I cleaned up the blood that was visible to the eye and left well enough alone. I had to wipe off everything I could remember touching which I had kept to a minimum as it was. I cut Candy up into sections in the tub. I separated her limbs, torso, hips and head and put them into some large black trash bags to put in my trunk.

I finishing packing the rest of her body into my trunk and walked back into my room forgetting the time when I heard a knock on the door. *Shit, it had been over four hours and this must be someone checking up on them.* I hadn't watched earlier to see if I had been followed. *Fuck, how could I be so careless?* I was getting cocky that's what it was. I looked out of the peephole in the door and someone had their finger on it from the other side. I waited silently hoping they would just go away. No luck, there was another knock and when I ignored it again whoever was on the other side kicked the door, attempting to bust it open. I put my foot in front of it trying to hold it shut but he kicked it again catching me off guard and knocking me back, opening the door. It was the beefy Mexican pimp. He saw Violet dead on the bed and instantly rushed me. "She was my top bitch," he said while grabbing for me. "Where's the other one?"

I pointed and looked quickly to the side to throw him off guard and when he looked where I wanted him to I clocked him hard with the back of my balled up fist right in the temple. I had prepared myself for this kind of shit since I was young so there wasn't much he could do besides try until he failed. He stepped back stunned and I gave him no other chances, I punched him hard in the throat. He fell back a bit tears starting to fill up his eyes causing a lack of vision. I took my opportunity and as he stepped back I rushed forward and brought my elbow with all my weight and force down onto the top of his head. He dropped to his knees and it was over. I closed the door quickly and then hit him again with another hard elbow while he was stunned knocking him out cold. I then started to squeeze his neck harder than any neck from before. I heard it pop in seconds and I kept on squeezing it, before long I realized that my fingers were bloody from digging into his skin. If I kept squeezing like that I felt I might have popped his head off, my anger had taken over. Good thing I had shut the door earlier.

I finally realized what this was all about, Violet had given him a signal to follow and I had not been paying all that much attention. I felt bad for him, the poor guy just wanted to do his job, making money off his girls and I had murdered his entire business in one shot. I tried to come to grips with what I was doing with my life. I couldn't figure out if I was alright or if I was just crazy.

Where was my wise tree from all those dreams I used to have? I needed some answers. Something that made me feel so bad lately wasn't anything I wanted a part of anymore. I was seriously debating whether or not to stop killing people for a while. I felt like I needed to tame the beast before it got too far out of its cage. I didn't even have a direction anymore besides trying to fill the loneliness with murder. Lately that had become my entire life. Even people eating human flesh against their wills didn't excite me anymore. I needed to curb the appetite to kill or I felt I might lose my soul.

XXI.

About two months later I was taking a walk in the sand along the beach. I liked to walk along the waters edge in the night and just think while smoking a joint. I found it helped if I wanted to curb my cravings to kill. I had a joint that I wanted to smoke in a little plastic container I brought with me. It wasn't that I wanted to kill people all of the time or anything, I just had an easier time not giving in when I smoked. I could smoke a nice joint and I would forget about it and just enjoy myself.

I was literally about to light it up when I was approached from behind by a crazy wide eyed white thug in a bundled up flight jacket. He had on a gray Russian style winter hat with thick straps that hang down the sides and he had a black bandana over his face as if he were attempting a stage coach robbery in the Old West. As he moved closer to me and I could see his eyes were bright blue and they looked very familiar to me. They weren't quite the same but I could see the same desperate look the meth head had in his eyes. If he was trying to rob me I could imagine he did other things to people and who knows how far he would take it in the future. I couldn't quite see who he was since he was wearing the bandana over his face but I stared directly into his eyes and held his gaze as intensely as I could. I wanted him to be unsure of himself, so that he might make a mistake.

He yelled at me, "GIVE ME YOUR WALLET!" waving a small buck knife in my face. I put the joint behind my ear. I didn't look away from his eyes as I reached back and took my wallet out of my pocket. I was amused that this was happening to be honest. It was like getting a little taste of my own medicine but I was still a little annoyed that I hadn't even gotten to take a toke or two before he came along. I was feeling those old urges trying to resurface. I held my wallet out to the side of me waving it just a little bit out of his reach. "I'M FUCKING SERIOUS!" he screamed in a raspy low voice as if he wanted to sound tough but didn't want to be heard by anyone else nearby.

I didn't move. I just held the wallet and stared at him not saying a word. He started to sway his gaze looking around for signs of anyone that might see us, or an escape route. He was becoming visually nervous now. His eyes were dodgy and he was shifting side to side on his feet. I wanted to make sure whether or not there were going to be witnesses. I took this opportunity to survey my surroundings as well…there was nobody in sight. He was still distracted and looked too far to his left once. Quick as a flash I grabbed the knife out of his hand leaving him standing there, shocked and unsure what to do. He had just lost all of his power.

I reached out to grab him by the neck and choke him out so I could carry him down the sandy shore. I had a 4 wheeler with a small trailer of sorts attached to the back of it parked a ways down the beach. I had a surfboard on the top and some various other beach ready tools in it as well. The interior was red for obvious reasons but if anyone happened to get a glimpse inside it wouldn't look anything out of the ordinary. I had a fish net inside of it as well as a life preserver just incase I needed to be helpful sometime. I didn't want anyone thinking twice about the fact that I could be finding people and hauling them off in it like the last time I had been out here. I just bring it in case someone happens to give me that old familiar feeling, like this time.

I happened across a beachgoer one late night before I decided to quit killing for a while. He was a young yuppie type. He was actually a part of the reason that I now smoked joints on the beach. I happened upon this guy trying to light one up and I interrupted him. I made sure to smoke the rest of the joint that he didn't get to finish.

The look on his face when I took the joint out of his mouth was priceless. He offered me some money and I let him know I had other things on my mind. I probably wasn't the guy he wanted to share his last joint with, but it happened. I felt a cold wind over my shoulder for a while after that happened. It was one reason that I wanted to quit killing that helped me stop. He may have been an asshole but I don't think he really deserved to die. It felt off. I felt a little bit like that night when I tripped in front of Lucas. Like the stars themselves were pulling for me to fail that night or maybe just that I had to work harder for it. It was just a moment that stuck with me now more than others. I didn't have to work for it I overpowered him quite easily. I probably wouldn't kill that guy again if I had a chance to do it over. So I like to remember like this, smoking in his honor.

It had been so long since I had lost it I almost thought about letting my attempted robber go. Something told me he would probably do this again and next time probably hurt someone that didn't deserve it. I had laid off of the killing myself for that reason so I felt justified this time. As I reached for his neck, he stepped back and tried to duck down so instead of grabbing his neck, I grabbed the front of his bandana and ripped it down as he stepped back again. What I saw stopped me dead. He saw his moment and took it to run away into the shadows of the night. This was a guy that I had never known in life but I would never forget his face.

It was a face from my dreams as a kid. I remembered seeing his face vividly sitting in my future self's refrigerator. I'll never forget it because he was missing his eyes. It was like every time I felt like my life was going off course, I would get a reminder somehow of my dreams. Like something was telling me I was on the path I was supposed to be on.

This guy, unfortunately for him, was also a person who should not have imbibed the devil's toxin, he ran fast, but not fast enough to catch me off of my guard. I followed him in silent pursuit waiting for my chance to strike. He didn't even look back which told me that he had never even thought twice about me following him. I caught him a quarter mile down the beach where it was nice and almost pitch black. The sound of the small waves reaching their end drowned out my footsteps as I approached him from behind. I jumped up when I was close enough and came down with all of my weight, my elbow solidly landing on the top of his head. He dropped instantly and I was absolutely sure he wasn't going to wake up for a few minutes at the least. My vehicle wasn't far away so I tied his hands to his feet with his own shoelaces and gagged him. He was drunk and knocked out so it probably wasn't necessary but I felt better anyways. I flung him over my shoulder and carried him back to my trailer to take back to my house.

When he woke up he had a knot on his head and a pounding headache, judging from the way he squinted his eyes and peeled his lips back. He looked like someone who just got flashed in the eyes right before a picture was snapped. I put a pan over his head smacking it with a large heavy metal screwdriver I had brought from the garage creating a loud crashing noise that vibrated the air around us. His eyes rolled back into his head as the pain hit him and he pleaded "Stop! You're going to blow my head up!"

I laughed at him, "Who are you to order me around?"

"Just another asshole who works to pay me when I come robbing. You're lucky I didn't have my gun tonight or you would have been shot." He said matter of factly. He was tied up and vulnerable, so my guess was that he had just seen one too many Dirty Harry movies and saw some outcome I didn't in this. He was after all trying to be a tough guy, in MY basement... with ME of all people.

I wanted to show him that was a bad idea. "Stick out your tongue." I told him.

"Fuck you. Make me stick out my tongue." came his not so smart reply.

I took a pair of pliers out of my back pocket and showed them to him. He still refused to open his mouth. I showed him a screwdriver that was like a crowbar I had. It was over a foot long and a weighed a few pounds. He looked at it and shrugged his shoulders as if to say "Yeah, so?" I flicked my wrist flipping the screwdriver around so I was holding the metal end. Then with the handle, I came down with all the force I could manage. The screwdriver broke his jaw on one side and after a couple of swings he couldn't hold it together anymore. I stuck my fingers inside of his mouth and ripped open his jaw about six inches more than it should have opened.

I had never done that before and it was surprising how elastic the face can be. His screams of agony filled my basement. I didn't worry that anybody would hear him. My closest neighbor Steve was working and nobody else was close enough to worry me, especially in the midnight hours. I used the pliers as he tried to move his head back and forth and reached into his open mouth and gripped onto his tongue. He didn't even try moving now out of fear. He was probably hoping that I would be merciful if he didn't fight with me right now. He was wrong. I pulled his tongue out as far as I could with my pliers and cut out as much of his tongue as I could with the buck knife that I snagged from his hand earlier.

I moved in front of him and stared at him until he looked into my eyes. "Are you done now?" He gave me one of the meanest glares I had ever been given. If looks could kill, I would have been a dead son of a bitch right then.

I couldn't believe the defiance even now in his eyes. I went to the kitchen to get a teaspoon from the drawer and walked back in to stand in front of him, holding it out for him to see. He looked at the spoon for a second and then looked back at me and I could almost see the question mark forming over his head. I grabbed his forehead and pushed his head back using my powerful arms to hold him still. He was secured to the chair and couldn't move anything besides his head which right now wasn't going to work. I eased the spoon into the socket behind his terrified eye nice and slow. He never had a chance to stop it from happening.

I could hear the fluids making a squishing noise as the spoon separated the muscle from muscle. A clearish red liquid leaked out from the newly formed space in his eye socket. Part of it was blood but it was being thinned out by something else. I could hear the bones in his face chattering as he tried shaking his head out of my grip as his broken jaw bones smacked together. There was a lot of fear in his desperate screams now but I saw anger in the other eye, or so I told myself as I proceeded to dig out the other eyeball. I hated to leave a job half finished.

Halfway through the second eyeball, he quit trying to scream and passed out cold. At least I thought he passed out, but when I checked his pulse, he was off the radar of the living. I must have scared him to death because he hadn't lost enough blood to have died from the wounds. Maybe the pain was just that intense that it shut down his faculties. Either way I cut his head off and stuck it in my freezer. I decided to make a soup and when I put the eyes into it I had to laugh. I realized that this was an exact scenario from the dreams I had as a child. I had to wonder if it was more than just a dream and I was indeed a child again looking through the tree at my future self, eating the eyeballs from this very soup so long ago.

I looked towards the area I remembered watching from, trying to spot something like a transparent blur or even a barely visible shadow or fuzzy space like you might imagine if you were to see a ghost or something. Some sort of light would be cool, anything that would answer my questions.

Unfortunately, I couldn't see anything of the sort but I swore if I listened hard enough, for a moment… I could hear the sound of my younger self vomiting.

XXII.

This not killing people thing was becoming harder for me every day. I had way too many reminders around my house that I decided I just needed to get rid of. I had all of my skulls and other body parts in my garage. I had already gone through most of the meat from my despicable mugger. I was beginning to feel like I needed more. Sometimes I would look at people and I would see their muscles throbbing as they went about their business. I would think about how delicious they could be as my teeth ripped through a thick steak of them. I had been caught a couple of times staring with my mouth hanging open and once or twice I had to physically wipe drool from my face.

I had a lady once who gave me a nasty look and walked away mumbling something about my being a pervert when she caught me looking at her ass and drooling. She had no idea… This was more than just a craving, I was addicted. There was definitely something in human meat that my body had gotten used to and I was missing now. I felt like I was trying to stay clean off of coke or something and there was all kinds of it everywhere. I was afraid to eat what I had left and had been sparing it as much as I could lately but it was starting to backfire on me now. Maybe it was mental but I felt weak when I didn't eat it every day.

Luckily a body lasts quite a while when it's just me consuming it. Even when I had done the barbeques I hadn't even used up an entire body, now I felt low when I had half of one left. Life would be much simpler if I didn't have this problem. I had heard stories about an insatiable hunger that comes with cannibalism. I never truly believed it until I became a cannibal and ran out of the delicacy that was man. It feels like your hunger can never be fully satisfied with any other meat once you go down that road. Nothing but Homosapien sandwiches or soup a la people will leave your stomach feeling truly satisfied.

Of course that's not 100 percent true, there are some delicious meats out there. There have been plenty of times I had eaten human flesh and gotten so overstuffed that I never wanted to eat another bite of mankind again. Exactly the same as an alcoholic who had just woke up from a regretful night of boozing. Or a heroin junkie after a blackout night of earning their next fix from the dealer. I'm here to tell you, feeling it now or feeling it later, the hunger does come up. I felt it horribly the emptier my refrigerator got. If I was ever truly going to stop, I would have to go cold turkey.

Lately my mind felt clouded, I wasn't sure about anything anymore. It was uncomfortable to me. To tell the truth, I was lucky I had gotten away with this for nearly two decades already. I felt that a good house cleansing was the best plan of action for me now. I cried as I packed away all of my parts and memories into my trunk. I found a nice little boat off of the internet so that I could take all of my murder memorabilia and dump it into a permanent watery grave. I had one final meaty dinner left. It was a nice rump steak from the thug I had last killed. It was a fitting end to my cannibalism, the last chop of the last chop. When I was done, I headed off into the night to take everything to the boat.

I was driving down the street listening to the radio when an announcement broke in about some previous murder being investigated so I turned it up. They had some new information on an old murder but they couldn't give any more details. For some reason that news broadcast gave me the chills. How many people were listening to that who might have to worry? I didn't know any besides me and it just didn't feel right. Before I could settle myself down and straighten my head out, I noticed some blue and red lights coming from my rearview and bouncing off of the interior of my car. I had been zoning out and forgot to keep my foot on the gas pedal. I was only going about 20 in a 45 mph zone and I was being pulled over.

I couldn't help it, I began physically shaking against my best efforts. I had body parts in my trunk from at least twelve different victims and was nervous already from the news about the murder. I couldn't think of anything specifically I had forgotten or left behind but sometimes I didn't really pay attention to all the things that I probably should, to err is human. It's a cocky move on my part I know but over the years there had been times I felt untouchable. Now was not one of them.

First of all, they had mentioned that they didn't have the suspect in custody and here I was carrying evidence in my trunk and getting pulled over. What if they ran my name and I had a warrant for my arrest? Of all the shitty times to be pulled over, it had to be while I was transporting the parts of all my victims to get rid of them. The skulls that were in my trunk were all boiled clean and painted over but they still weren't medical issue. Not to mention that I wasn't medically certified to have them and that was required for them to be legal. I had to take a couple of deep breaths trying to calm myself down. I couldn't afford to let this all go down just because I was going to slow or freaking out.

A lady cop came to my window and signaled for me to roll down my window with her finger in a circular motion. I rolled it down hoping she would just give me a ticket and let me go on my way. "License and registration." she said. I took my time looking in the glovebox, hoping she would just let me off with a warning. "Do you know why I pulled you over?" she asked.

I was relieved; some kind of automatic calm had taken over as she stood there, I was no longer shaking. "Yeah officer, I'm sorry I was trying to set my cruise control and it wasn't working. I'm assuming I was going to slow?" She shined a light into my car and looked around. I held my license up near the steering wheel pretending not to pay much attention to her. I couldn't let her run my name. If this was about me there would be a swarm of cop cars here before I could blink. With all this evidence in my trunk there would be no way I would ever see the light of day again.

She wasn't paying as much attention as she probably should have been and when she reached in for my license with her right hand I grabbed it quickly and in one swift motion yanked her inside my window over my lap. When she was on my lap before she had much chance to do or say anything I hit her in the back of the head with a solid blow, knocking her out instantly. I pulled her the rest of the way in and sat her in the passenger seat as if she were just sleeping. Her head rolled to the side. I was careful to hold her down out of sight. As far as I could tell nobody was around who could have seen anything, so I took her with and drove to the boat.

I had officially let myself go. I reached my boat and loaded everything onto it. I moved her first before anyone was around to see anything. There were a couple of boats out on the water but they were too far away to be able to see anything. I made sure to tie her hands and feet up securely and bound her mouth so she couldn't scream. She probably wouldn't want to anyways because I'm sure her head will be throbbing when she wakes up. I started the boat and began driving towards the open ocean while listening to her police radio from her belt.

After about 5 minutes of unrelated chatter they called her to ask for a report. When they had no answer their queries for her became a bit more frantic. She gave no answer and I could hear the worry in their voices. Another officer was sent to her car by dispatch. All of the police cars were tracked by gps in case someone might try and steal one of them or an officer goes missing. After about 10 minutes there was a positive response that her car was indeed there but that she was gone. They tried calling her again on her radio. I didn't answer. Dispatch said for the officer to bring in the memory stick from the camera in the cruiser, so they could review it and see if that gave them any new information.

I could literally feel my face go green. How could I have forgotten about something that important!? I had in my panic completely forgotten that police cars had dash cams. I suddenly felt sick so I stopped the motor letting the boat float for a bit while I vomited violently over the side of it. I hadn't puked like that in a long time. I couldn't believe on the day I decided to try doing the right thing for once that everything could go so wrong.

I heard her trying to mumble something from the floor of the boat and I felt that old familiar rage boiling up. I was completely fucked now. I bent down to her and her eyes grew wide with fear as I grabbed her by the hair and threw her against the side of the boat. I know that my size frightened her by the way she cowered from me. Tears began streaming down her face as she tried to plead through the gag in her mouth. I stared at her for a minute letting myself feel the fear and intense emotions coming from her as she realized that these may well be her last moments alive.

The fact that I probably would have just gotten a ticket before and been on my way saddened me. Instead, I had panicked and kidnapped an officer of the law. What was worse was that I had done it in front of her dash cam on the cruiser. I was so ashamed of myself. I couldn't believe I had been this careless. I was out of control and I didn't think I could stop no matter how badly I wanted to. I couldn't leave her alive though. I pulled her to me against her feeble attempts to fight it being tied up and terrified. I put her in the old familiar crease of my elbow and began to cut off the blood and air to her body. After about 10 seconds she went limp. Another 10 seconds and she started to shake in short bursts as her skin turned darker and she started to die from lack of blood and oxygen.

I started to cry. I couldn't help it. I let the tears stream down my face as I felt her shaking in my arms as her life spit the last energies it ever would through her dying muscles. When she finally stopped I dropped her down and fell down on top of her sobbing harder than before now that I didn't have to hold her still. As I lay on her chest my weight pushed out the stale remaining air that she had in her lungs and I felt her last warm breath gently blow against my face. I hugged her dead body as if I could offer her any comfort but what I really wanted was to die with her.

What was to be next? I would start killing children or innocent old people on the streets at night? I couldn't live with that. This was the epitome of what I didn't want to become. I looked at her still body lying there still gagged, her hands tied behind her back. Her tears were drying on her face under her now empty eyes. I saw she still had her belt on and I noticed the black case that was holding her state issued pistol. I grabbed the gun from her clip on her belt as if in a trance, I breathed a few deep breaths the strange calm coming back over me again. When I felt relaxed again, I lowered my head, brought the gun up to my forehead… and shot myself in the third eye.

XXIII.

I was completely shocked when I woke up. It was amazing enough that I had woken up in the first place but I wasn't supposed to still be alive. As I looked around, I realized that I was inside of the nightmare forest once again. I was a bit apprehensive at first but when I looked around this time, there weren't bloody organs and body parts strung all through the trees and on the ground. Instead it was just a nice warm day.

The sun was out and I could hear birds singing and sounds of life reverberating all around me. It meant that there was life after death and I finally had no reason to fear it. In death there was something different about the forest; besides the fact that there was no more squishy wet ground soaked in blood. Everything looked and felt great, as if the nightmare was actually over for real. I felt at peace for a moment and my troubles from life were seeming farther away with each passing moment.

After a while of walking through the forest enjoying the beauty and solitude of it I came across a familiar looking tree. I hadn't seen it in the light before but it looked to be THE tree rooted right in front of me. Although it was just a tree, all gnarled and old, it still felt like it was a wise being and could see right through me. I suddenly felt afraid. I was ashamed at how things wound up in the end and feared what the tree might show me this time.

The tree didn't move. It didn't say anything in its booming voice or try to put me inside of itself; it just sat there like any other every day tree. I have to admit I was kind of disappointed. I decided to climb inside of the tree on my own this time just to see what was in it when there was enough light to see. I crawled inside of it and my feet hit the bottom inside the enormous hole. I looked up and oddly it seemed too dark to see the walls inside of it.

I looked out of the large hole in front of me and I could see dark clouds forming above the barely visible treetops. They began coming together slowly at first and then like a freak storm, clouds darkened the entire sky. It was an ominous feeling and that feeling was all I could concentrate on. I looked around and soon I couldn't see much more than five feet around me on any side. I tried to turn around to go back out but the exit seemed to have vanished from where it had just been a moment ago.

I started to get a little scared now that I couldn't just wake up from a dream and be okay. This could turn out to be an eternal nightmare! I heard the booming voice from all around me now. It thundered: "THE BLOOD MAKES IT REAL." Suddenly, what seemed like 1000 TV screens turned on all around me, each one of them showing different scenarios in what looked to be scenes from random people's lives.

In each situation I looked at and concentrated on the sound would tune in like a radio station. Instead of static though, it would go from silence to crystal clear sound. In one of the streams of video there was a pregnant woman who was in labor. I could see the skin on her stomach moving from the babies hand underneath. The sweat from her overheated body covered her whole stomach and dripped from her face. As she was pushing to try and get the baby out of her, a large, rubber gloved hand came down thrusting a gigantic butcher knife into her stomach. The look on her face said she hadn't seen that coming. I could hear her bloodcurdling screams as I looked away in disgust.

I was glad that it wasn't showing me things I was supposed to do in the future, I was after all dead. I looked around again, curious and hoping for a better show than that sick shit. I spotted another scene with a guy in a truck screaming at a crying baby boy that was just seat belted in on the seat. There was no car seat and it kept falling over as the guy drove like shit. It was probably barely standing or walking and not quite strong enough to withstand the forces of motion like he was being put through right now. He had a beer in his cup holder near the ashtray and he took a long swig off of it. The baby had a red, swollen face from what looked like being backhanded or punched. The poor thing was crying and the guy was screaming at it to stop.

In a rage, he stomped on his brakes, making the truck skid to a screeching halt on the side of the highway. He walked around to the other side of the truck and pulled the scared baby out by one of its legs and slammed it onto the street, knocking the wind out of him. Then with all the weight he could muster, he raised his leg high into the air and stomped on its little head so hard his skull bones crushed instantly with a sickening pop.

"What the fuck is this bullshit?" I said to the tree as if it would converse with me on a personal level. "Are all of these scenes that fucked up?" I looked at another one and it seemed to be alright. Everybody in it was laughing and having a good time, which was something I wanted to see. I felt that I had seen and done enough evils for several lifetimes and I didn't want to see any more right now. I looked at this screen with delight because it was a break from the death and destruction that was being displayed all around me.

Just when I was starting to feel a little better the door to the room they were having a party in flew open and a man came in opening fire on the party with an automatic assault rifle. I then saw it was a wedding party and knew that this guy wasn't ready to let his ex-marry someone else. I watched as he blasted a 2nd shot into his ex and her new husbands heads and then put it to his chin and pulled the trigger.

"Fuck!" I screamed looking desperately for anything that wasn't evil. It became apparent all too soon that on every screen was a murder more horrific than the last and there was going to be no escape. If I just tried to close my eyes it would be as if I had transparent eyelids all of a sudden and I would see the scenes vividly as if it were my own imagination or memories. I deserved this. I knew that now, maybe this was hell. My own personal hell and I was going to have to see this shit for eternity when all I want is to sleep and forget my problems.

I had killed myself. I had ended the life that was given to me because I couldn't maintain control of myself. All of the televisions instantly shut off when I finished that thought. I could hear faint voices surrounding me in the darkness. I couldn't hear what they were saying, just their whispering. I couldn't see anything either, once again it was back to darkness. It was a darkness that had become absolute. There were no lights, no smells, nothing but the darkness beyond my eyes and the faint voices.

"Life is precious," I heard them saying all at once like a perfectly harmonized crowd of people. All of a sudden I had thousands of pictures flying through my head, all vivid and all slowed down and although I know it was just seconds that went by it seemed much longer. I could see so many people, all smiling and all oblivious, all just, being. There was nothing sad or weird about these visions flowing through my head. I could sense that it was supposed to be that way. Life was meant to be full of love and laughter and connections. I hadn't truly connected with anybody in my life. It was all empty and lonesome. I could feel the emotions these people had for each other and the genuine emotion flowing from them and it was making me feel more like they were. I could feel the darkness that was consuming me starting to fade away. I could see people hugging one another, loving each other and just being human.

I felt a huge wave of regret sweep over me. There was no life that was worth more than another, what I had been doing is just killing to kill. I let myself spin way out of control and that was dangerous. I could now feel the joy of these people; I could feel their frailties and their humanity. I was ashamed that I had preyed on innocent people at all. I felt like less of a man every day. Life was all fake smiles and obsessions nobody knew about. I felt even worse though for taking my own life. I could now see just how precious human life could be and I had just wasted mine by my own hand.

An overwhelming surge of emotion suddenly hit me and I started to cry. Slowly at first, then it turned into a body shaking sob and I almost felt like I couldn't stop if I wanted to. The more I tried to stop the worse my sobbing became. I let it go and before I knew it I was in the fetal position bawling like a baby. I thought of all the innocent people I had taken away from living and poor Lucas, before he even knew what-was-what, I had murdered him and his father. Worst of all was the fact that his beautiful innocent mother had killed herself and I had been the catalyst. She was probably going to want to kill me if she ever saw me again. I was guessing that if I was still conscious, there was a good chance that she and Lucas and his father might be as well.

After what seemed like an hour of crying, I felt a tremendous pain in my midsection. I hadn't noticed in my sorrow but the tree had grabbed me and was squeezing me very hard now. I couldn't breathe or move or loosen its grip in the slightest. I tried prying with my hands and pushing with my feet, but it might as well have been made out of steel because nothing I did seemed to work, in fact it only made the tree squeeze me tighter.

I tried to yell for forgiveness, "I'm sorry, please. I don't want to die." I thought I was already dead, but I could feel my bones cracking under the tremendous power of its grip and I felt like I was suffocating, unable to breathe. I was becoming more convinced by the second that if I wasn't dead already, the tree planned on killing me. It squeezed harder than before and I could feel the pressure on my ribs becoming too much and a couple of my ribs cracked and snapped.

I tried to cry out but I couldn't breathe let alone use my diaphragm to scream. All I could do was sit there helpless, unable to lose consciousness and hoping the tree would let me go. I felt more like I was going to die now than before when I actually did die. After what seemed like an eternity, the tree gave a final squeeze and I could feel all my bones in my chest and back finally snap under the pressure.

I was pretty sure that my lungs had exploded or were at least pierced by some of my ribs, yet somehow I couldn't pass out. I was choking, unable to catch a breath. I had never wanted anything as badly as I wanted to pass out right now but I had no choice other than to deal with the pain and anguish. I just hoped that it wouldn't last forever.

The booming voice said, "YOU'RE NOT A VICTIM! QUIT FEELING SORRY FOR YOURSELF. YOU CHOSE THIS, TO BE AN INSTRUMENT OF CHANGE. THE BLOOD MAKES IT REAL!"

I could barely gasp out, "The blood… makes… what real?" I was tired of these half answers. I could barely catch enough air in my lungs to get that out. I needed to relax but every time I tried to settle my broken body I would receive sharp pains that were almost worse than if I just held myself up.

There was silence for a minute and then the booming voice again echoed by the strange whispers all around me. Together they emphasized and I could easily understand what they were saying to me. "THE PURPOSE OF YOUR EXISTENCE IS MURDER, PURIFICATION THROUGH THE DESIRES OF THE FLESH. HUMANS ARE WEAK, WE SHED YOUR PURITY FROM A YOUNG AGE. YOU KILL THOSE WHOS TIME IS UP, NOTHING MORE. BEYOND THAT IS OF NO

CONSEQUENCE, ENDING LIVES IS YOUR PURPOSE, IT'S THE REASON YOU EXIST." I finally understood what it meant, rather, I was shown.

I thought that I had been killing people just because I was losing my mind, I had more than a few times questioned my own motives trying my hardest to hold onto my last shred of humanity. Every time I did I was shown repeated dreams of unspeakable horrors in order to be desensitized and switch my attention back to the goal at hand. I wasn't sure why I hadn't been told this earlier before I ended my life but I suspected I probably wouldn't have believed it anyways. As far as I was concerned back then there was no afterlife. When I took a life it was gone. After all I had never had experiences with ghosts or anything of that nature. That was the reason I looked for souls after a kill.

I felt much better knowing I had not killed the wrong people at least. Even those I thought were innocent; it was just their time to go. Then there were those who needed to die for the greater good. For instance, the child molester I had trapped and killed was going to murder a dozen children over the course of the next five years if left to go about it as he wanted. Those kids would have all died prematurely and one little boy in particular was supposed to be highly influential in ways the world desperately needed.

There was a time and place for people to die and it's all chosen before we're even born. There are however different paths to take during a life. Each can affect your life in a different way, taking you down a different path each time, with each decision. I was an instrument of death like the grim reaper that would help people along specific paths according to how things were going. The junkie I had killed had already raped plenty of innocent women high on drugs and had actually killed a couple others, only he was never found out. The girlfriend he had beaten was going to die the night she came home. She would have been a victim of a drug overdose as he pushed her to shoot some up. When she died, he was going to have another girl the next night not even skipping a beat. She would also end up dead and the pattern would begin again. The wannabe hoodlum I had killed and eaten that tried to rob me, was becoming fed up with life and was going to shoot up a mall later on in that week, killing lots of innocent people.

I was naturally attracted to these people because it was meant for me to kill them. The ways I did it were my choice but I still had a hard time believing that I was an instrument of good that had to do bad things. I felt the sadness come over me as I thought about the dead cop. I still didn't feel that she deserved to die, but the tree was done answering me. I was losing control there was no doubt about that. That's why there had been mistakes of course, the whores I had killed didn't necessarily deserve death and come to think of it they weren't as tasty as I would have liked. *At least it's over.* I thought. I would do it all better if I got the chance. Knowing what I know now, I would have kept it under control. This was a bigger picture than the laws of earth. This was life according to the Gods of reality.

As I lay there in the dark, I was suddenly aware that I couldn't feel the pain anymore and I was feeling extremely tired. In fact, I was feeling more tired than I had ever felt in my entire life. I suddenly couldn't keep my eyes open. I felt like maybe this was going to be it. I was going to die for real this time. I closed my eyes and drifted off to sleep unable to help myself. I didn't dream a thing.

XXIV.

When I woke up this time, I was lying in a bed. I couldn't move my arms or legs and I had a very hard time opening my eyes. The light seemed way too bright and my eyes were thumping a steady pain to the back of my head. My first thought was that somehow I had survived the suicide and was just paralyzed by the tree. That wasn't possible though since in reality I had only ever seen the tree in my dreams. I tried calling out for someone that could answer some questions but my throat was so full of phlegm and stale saliva that I couldn't get much more than a raspy cough out.

When I finally coughed some of the phlegm loose I could immediately taste it. It tasted as you would imagine dust to taste, only it was wet dust and had a mossy edge to it. I started to gag, it must have been a while since I had been able to do that but I was sure it had been sitting there growing nastier as I slept. I must have been here for a while, if I had indeed survived the suicide I was afraid to see what I looked like. I could think just fine but I couldn't move my body. It was like my muscles had become so weak that I couldn't get them to do anything. As if my brain had lost the signal to my body.

Finally, after what felt like a confusing eternity of immobile pain and numbness, I managed to croak out a weak "Hello?" I was surprised at the sound of my own voice. It cracked and stung quite a bit also making me wonder if I had gotten some kind of shrapnel from the bullet that somehow ricocheted into my throat.

I heard the sound of hard heeled shoes clicking on the tile of the floor as someone was coming towards me. I heard a woman saying excitedly, "I think I just heard him. I think he's awake!" I looked up as my eyes were finally adjusting to the brightness and I saw a middle aged graying nurse gazing down at me. She was smiling at me as if I didn't bother her at all. I'll bet she wouldn't be smiling if she knew about the cop I had murdered before I shot myself. In fact all I saw in her eyes was excitement that I was waking up. She seemed genuinely pleased.

What the fuck was going on?

"I am so glad to see you awake!" She said. "There are a lot of other people who are going to be happy to see you awake as well."

I'm sure she was talking about the cops. No way that I would think I was going to get away with it after all of the evidence I had left including a bullet in the brain from the gun of the cop I had dispatched. The nurse squeezed my hand warmly and walked away in a hurry smiling from ear to ear excited to go and let whoever she was talking about know I was awake. I drifted back off to sleep for a while before I was woken up by scattered voices around me.

One of the voices in particular sounded very familiar, she was saying "Oh please God let him wake up, don't let him be asleep for so long again!" It sounded like she was in a panic and it piqued my interest so I slowly opened my eyes and looked up. I could see my mother's face silhouetted in the fluorescent lights behind her. She looked so much younger than I remembered her being the last time I had seen her. She was staring down at me with all the love a mother would show for her son.

I was still confused that I didn't have an army of police around me. Did they not get the video feed after all? If they had found me and brought me here, the dead cop would have been right there lying next to me on that boat. Yet here was my mother looking down at me as lovingly as the day I was born and she had joyful tears flooding her eyes.

I figured that the tree must have done a number on me, or the bullet must have come close but hadn't hit its mark. I remembered the loud explosion and the feeling of pressure as I saw a flash of bright white light up my head… and then nothingness until I woke up in the forest. There was no pain, just a loss of consciousness as if I was knocked out and woke up inside of a dream. Just as I was thinking about that my mother told me, "I'm so happy, my little boy is finally awake." She raised her hands up over her mouth as her eyes dropped a surprising amount of tears.

"Little boy," I said to her. "I haven't been a little boy for a long time now. Thank you for the compliment though." I tried to muster the best smile I could manage for her. She looked a little worried when I said that but didn't say anything. "When do I get to go home then?" I asked her. I was fishing for an answer as to what they knew but she looked at me with a soft smile still.

"Well, you can come home as soon as they're sure the coma is not going to hit you again."

"Probably at least a couple of nights." The nurse chimed in giving me a rehearsed smile and going about with her business, letting us talk.

"Don't worry, I didn't need you to worry about me, I'll be fine. I'm awake now and other than feeling pins and needles when I try to move, I think I'll be okay." I told her matter of factly. I didn't want her to worry; she already looked like she had lost enough sleep. She looked at me with that stubborn look a mother will give when you know that you are going to lose the argument. She looked at the nurse who looked back at me and gave a reassuring smile as if she had seen this a thousand times.

"Don't worry; the confusion will wear off after a bit. He has been in a coma for 4 months." The nurse said. She rubbed my head like an aunt would do to a kid. I didn't even notice right away because I was trying to understand if I had heard her correctly.

"Can someone tell me what the hell is going on?" I was starting to feel like I was in the Twilight Zone. "I'm a grown man; don't treat me like a kid." The nurse chuckled, as did my mother.

My mother asked, "What's the last thing you remember?"

"I was driving my boat and I got into an accident." I didn't mention the passenger because it wasn't being brought up by anyone else and I knew better than to direct attention to something I wanted left alone.

She looked at me oddly again and said, "You dreamt you were driving a boat?" I opened my mouth to say something and decided against it. This trying to converse wasn't getting me anywhere. "That bottle must have hit you harder than we thought it did."

"Mom, that was two decades ago!" I said. I was becoming more and more convinced that she had lost her mind.

My mother laughed and replied, "Umm no, that was 4 months ago." This time she was visibly wondering if I had gotten brain damage. I lifted my head forward the best I could and lifted my arm up with a tremendous effort. If I was 14, my arms would be much smaller.

"Don't move," said the nurse, trying to move towards me in case I fell off of the bed or something but I couldn't stop; I had to see for myself. I lifted up my arm and focused my vision against the blinding lights in the room. Sure enough, I had my little T-Rex arms back. Somehow, I was back in my 14 year old body. The room started spinning around me until everything went black and I almost passed out. I was back in a time when I had never shot myself, or killed anybody else for that matter. The tree crushing me had been a dream as well as my entire life had been up to this point. I still had memories of being a serial killer and I remembered what my mission was according to the tree. Was it possible I was being given a second chance, this time with the information I needed? If so then I was sent here for a reason and now I had a fresh start.

It had all been some supreme training from the entity tree of my nightmares. If this was indeed my second chance then this time, I would be able to handle it and handle it I would because after all…

THE BLOOD MAKES IT REAL.

The End

Preview of Life after dead. Part 2 in the Blood makes it real series. Coming soon!

Chapter 1

What the hell is wrong with me?

I could barely remember anything that happened to me more than a few days ago. Sometimes it was merely a few hours before my mind would turn a complete blank. I remembered seeing some very bright blinding lights. They were beautiful, more beautiful than any lights I had ever seen before... but before when?

I couldn't remember. My mind felt like it was scrambled. It was hard to keep my thoughts in any sort of semblance longer than a few seconds. Even trying to comprehend something seemingly simple like focusing, was enough to make my head hurt. I liked flashing colors and the reflections of lights bouncing off of shiny things but beyond that, I wasn't even sure what my own name was.

I needed to try and relax, my gut told me that much. I wanted to figure out exactly who I was and remember just what it was that I was trying to do but it seemed the more that I tried; the more difficult it got to think clearly about anything. Trying to define rhyme or reason for anything, paying any sort of focused attention and formulating complete sentences, were almost as alien to me as my life before these last few days.

I knew that I had somehow gotten myself here but I had this overwhelming sense that something was wrong and that being here was a mistake. I might as well have been trying to remember a dream I had as a child. To be honest, I think it would probably have been easier to do.

Out of the corner of my eye I saw a red triangular shape I had come to know all too well was just a pattern on the sleeve of my mother's shirt as she whisked by doing whatever she was busy with. She had on a white blouse with Swedish designs going up the sleeves and the bust. There were red triangular shapes on the sleeves with little white flowers on them. I could usually see her whizzing by out of the corners of my eyes as she would run around doing her thing.

She would smile at me as she passed by and it made me feel better every time. There was something a bit off about it though. My instinct told me there was a deep sadness inside of her that she was trying to hide from me.

I reached up to hug her almost automatically as if my body were programmed to do such things when I felt someone might need it. She laughed softly but with a little too much gusto as if she were trying to hold back a fit of hysteria in which she would start uncontrollably crying at any moment. She seemed to be alright though, opting instead to give in to the hug and show me that she loved me with every bit of warmth you would expect in an embrace like that. I still felt her sob a couple of times and when my shoulder grew warm I knew that she had left a couple of tears there.

"You know just when mommy needs a hug don't you handsome." She looked at me attempting to be strong for her and I could see the mixed pain and pride she had for me in the look on her face. It was almost a pity look as if she felt bad that I couldn't express myself the way I wanted to. She looked about how I felt at the moment. She rubbed my head affectionately and bent down to kiss my forehead.

I wanted to say "Yes I do, anything for you mother, you take great care of me when I can't do it myself."

I wanted to let her know how much I appreciated her and everything that she did for me in these last few days that I could barely remember. All that came out when I went for it was:

"You… care me, ma…" as I weakly pointed back at myself with a crooked finger held a little too close to my chest. I could feel a long warm string of drool fall onto my arm as I strung together that monstrosity of words and I quickly tried to slurp it back in. I was embarrassed at my lack of ability to portray my emotions in a moment like that. I wanted to make her feel better but all I think I was going to manage to do was to make her feel worse.

Amazingly, she understood what I was trying to say to her, or she had at least gotten the point. This was good because I was already starting to forget what it was we were even talking about now; having taken so much concentration to blurt out my nonsensical attempt at communication.

"I know baby, I will always take care of you too, so long as we both shall live." She had a far off look in her eyes as she reached forward to wipe the drool from my chin with her finger. "We've got each other, and that's all we'll ever need." She let out a long slow sigh and smiled weakly at me before kissing my head one more time. She stood up and pushed her chair in slowly seeming lost in thought. As she walked out of the room she folded her arms together in front of her as if she were closing a robe around herself.

If I was to be completely truthful, I had no memory of her before a few days ago. I know that sounds a little weird after all she was my mother, but there was definitely nothing I could tell you about her before these last few days. That didn't mean much technically since I couldn't remember anything about myself before this either but still, it struck me as odd. She was definitely a God-send for me, which I could never deny. She helped me with so much I don't know how I would be able to get along without her. She knew that It was frustrating for me to try and concentrate on anything long enough to accomplish it. I wasn't sure how to portray my feelings to her either, it seemed like my body just wasn't ready to cooperate with my brain.

I found quickly that if I needed something, I could just scream and she would come to the rescue. I would let out a long guttural sound from the depths of my abdomen and this miraculous woman would show up and take care of my needs as if she had done it a hundred times. Maybe she had, I didn't know, I just knew that I felt safe with her. As long as she was around I knew that I would be taken care of.

I looked down at the long oak table in the kitchen and I could see in front of me that I had been building things with Legos. You can use them to create virtually anything that you want to. I didn't seem to be making a very impressive structure from the looks of it, but I didn't mind. It was just something to keep my hands busy while I tried to think about where I had been before I woke up in the hospital. I remembered being able to articulate my thoughts without getting confused not very long ago. It seemed further away every day that passed but a few days ago I even knew who I was and what was going on but that quickly changed.

With each day that passed I seemed to be forgetting more and more about that first day. It seemed as if the knowledge of what was going on was whispering its secrets just quietly enough from the darkest recesses of my brain, that I couldn't hear what it was saying.

I was very frustrated not being able to remember anything. It didn't feel right that I was like this, or that I had been like this my entire life. The Dreadful Lego creation I had put together using my less than artful hands didn't help my mood either. It sort of resembled a car sitting on blocks like you might see in a low rent neighborhood. I took my left hand and swiped it onto the floor in a sudden fit of rage, the multi colored rectangles spilling onto the floor around the room.

Why couldn't I remember where I had been before the hospital? I felt like I was missing something. I understood that I wasn't a normal man as far as my intelligence level goes but why I could only remember a few days of my life I couldn't even begin to fathom and trying to ask anyone was a trivial waste of time. It seemed that everyone was smarter than me, or at least more articulate than I was. Whenever someone attempted to communicate with me, they would speak to me as if I were a foreigner from a faraway land who hadn't seen fit to learn English before they hopped on a boat to America. They all made sure to speak nice and slowly, almost as if I didn't have the capacity to understand them.

I had to admit though; sometimes it's nice not having to worry about impressing anyone. That thought relaxed me which was weird since I was so uncomfortable talking to people as it was. Just the thought that it was alright to be me, and nobody would judge me since they knew I was mentally deficient seemed to calm my nerves. I didn't really have the concentration to follow a conversation of average intelligence for very long without suddenly becoming completely confused as to what we were just talking about moments before.

Even my mother would sometimes catch herself speaking slower to me but would immediately stop herself when she realized she was doing it. She knew I needed her to slow down sometimes and would often make sure I was following her conversations by seeing how puzzled the looks on my face were becoming. I would feel my face flush and begin to frown and I could feel my eyebrows going up as if a question mark were trying to form on my forehead in the simplest of conversations. She always put forth her best efforts to be as nice as she could be to me. She never seemed to get upset or show me that I was frustrating her when she had to help me do things. I was very grateful that she was here for me and on my side.

I looked down at the mess of building blocks on the floor. My crappy creation that my mother told me was "A good job" was now broken into pieces. I picked them up quickly hoping in some small way that it would help keep her stress levels and sadness down. It wasn't fair to her that I could throw a fit and make such a mess and she should have to clean it up.

I had to stop for a second, I felt like that thought didn't belong in my mind, it seemed almost too smart to be from me. Usually my thoughts were more like pieces of a jigsaw puzzle desperately trying to fit together. Just as I had a thought I would forget what I was thinking about. It was hard to maintain my thoughts long enough to rationalize normally like most people could.

This was driving me crazy; I didn't want to be like this, unable to communicate. I wondered if I wasn't in some sort of accident. I certainly didn't feel like I was supposed to be a culmination of all the slow parts of my brain working together in a sickeningly pathetic unison. A couple of days ago I felt a lot closer to the answers I craved now than any other time since. I could remember what it felt like to be... smart. My mother acted like she had been doing this for years with me though and while she seemed on the verge of tears since I had woken up, I didn't think any of this was really new to her. The only problem was that she looked at me and saw someone familiar. When I would look into the mirror I saw someone else entirely as if it were the first time I was seeing myself. I couldn't recall ever looking into the mirror and seeing this face before. Like I was wearing a mask and looking at myself to see how I looked in it. Another thing that bothered me was if I've had this mother my entire life, why couldn't I remember her face before this? I couldn't recall one memory with her. Not one special day between us other than what I had come to experience these past few days.

When I first woke up and saw the doctor he said. "You had a seizure which put you into a coma. We thought you were never going to wake up again. Then just when we were about to give up hope and pull the plug, wouldn't you know it? There you were, as awake as the day before your seizure! You didn't recognize anybody, not even your mother and somehow you lost your entire memory, which was odd since you were born the way you were."

I suppose the doctor meant handicapped.

The first time that I laid my eyes on my mother I initially saw a look of excitement. Upon further scrutiny however there was an underlying look of pain hidden very well behind the guise of a smile. Once I spotted it, it was always there. Lately she always seemed to be crying until the moment she came into the room. Sometimes I would hear her sniffle and then there would be a brief pause before she would blow her nose, composing herself before coming into the area I was in. I hated being like this then, feeling so helpless when she was the one who really needed the help.

I started screaming in aggravation, rocking back and forth holding my hands over my ears. I thought that maybe those depressing thoughts wouldn't be there for her if I couldn't hear them in my own head. I must have rocked a little too hard because suddenly I lost my balance and fell backwards, hitting my head on the wall behind me with a sickening thud. I faded directly into dreamland in a flash of white that encompassed my head all at once as it made contact with the solid wall.

Chapter 2

I suddenly remembered a time that I was hanging out with a cousin of mine named Vincent; we used to call him Vinnie for short. We were all about 8 years old doing what all kids our age out here loved to do. We were swinging from a long old rope into the cool deep river, which was around a mile from my house. Vinnie decided this time that instead of just grabbing the rope and swinging into the water, he was going to ride his bike off the edge of the 10 foot cliff's edge and grab the rope in midair. We'd all jumped off of this cliff before on our bikes but none of us had tried to grab the rope as he was about to. We had all swung from the rope hundreds of times each and I knew, as well as every other kid who came out here that there was nothing to fear in this water. There were no rocks underneath it and no matter how you fell in; it was deep enough that you would most likely never touch the bottom unless you physically swam down. It seemed like a fun thing to watch and we were all for it, so we cheered him on.

Vinnie and I were there, as well as this cute little neighbor girl named Nikki that had a crush on Vinnie. She was a little Indian girl with big brown eyes and little dimples that when she smiled lit up her whole face. She liked to do things girls didn't normally do, making her very much a tomboy. Vinnie didn't mind that at all but he didn't really want to date her because from what he said she needed braces. Her teeth stuck out in spots like she had double sets of them and there wasn't room for them so a couple had grown outwards a bit. If you asked me though, they just added to the character of her face when she smiled. I think he was just too shy and she wasn't secretive about her crush.

As we cheered Vinnie on he started peddling as fast as he could, trying to get some speed for his jump. I looked around and saw everyone else smiling and watching him intently as he zoomed down the 20 foot path towards the edge of the cliff. He got to the edge and popped a wheelie jumping his front tire off the ledge and launched into the air. I watched him smile as if he were feeling the best rush ever…

Then things went horribly wrong.

He tried to grab the rope but his hands weren't able to grip it for more than maybe a half a second as his bike dropped to the water below. He lost his grip on the rope right afterwards, which caused his body to swing legs up face down. The bike splashed directly underneath him before his grip slipped leaving just enough time for him to fall headfirst directly on top of it before it could sink under. It didn't look good from where we were. I figured at first that he was going to hit his head on his bike and we would all laugh at him for being an idiot as he brought it back to the shore. He landed directly on the bike, head first. His head hit with a sickening pop entering a section in the frame just large enough to fit through and he was stuck. As his body flopped over we heard a loud crack, his body went limp and he and the bike sank under the water.

We sat there for a minute waiting for him to come up. When he didn't resurface, I jumped in to try and find him but when I reached where I thought he was I couldn't feel him or the bike at all. There was a slight current in the water that pulled you gently along that was easy to swim through to get back to the shore. If you let it take you and didn't swim it was strong enough to carry you for a ways in front of us and down the river. It got fast again about a quarter mile down. Nikki jumped in shortly after me, both of us swimming under the water trying to find him in a panic. Neither he nor the bike was anywhere near us and we decided not to waste any more time and sped off on our own bikes to get help.

I woke up from my self-inflicted unconsciousness screaming "My cousin! My cousin!"

Mother was holding my head in her hands saying, "Baby wake up, it's just a bad dream." I saw her big olive colored eyes looking at me very concerned now.

I said a little unsure this time, "My cousin." I couldn't remember my cousin very much now; it was quickly fading and becoming a distant memory.

Mother said, "You don't have a cousin honey. Mama never had a brother, or a sister. And as for your daddy, well you know that story already."

I didn't know what she meant. My mind wandered back to the hazy recollection of that seemingly nonexistent memory or dream I just had and I had to wonder how it could have been so clear. I could think straight somehow, as if I were remembering someone else's memories. Either way it was a relief to finally not be the stupid one, even if it wasn't real. It seemed so familiar though, and so vivid. It wasn't a very happy thing to have had happen though, watching that poor kid have his neck snap like that and then disappear. I was already starting to lose the memory and for once I was grateful for that, I wanted to try and forget it. I had stopped screaming for my cousin now and I just laid there in my mother's arms, feeling her warm, caring embrace; the violent memory drifting farther away every second.

I was almost asleep when I heard a solitary sniffle from my mother that made me jump a little. She squeezed me once more and kissed me on the forehead getting up to go make dinner. Dinner was what my mother referred to as my favorite, spaghetti. I couldn't remember spaghetti being necessarily my favorite but she was much smarter and had a much better memory than I did, so I trusted it. After all I had no idea what my favorite anything was.

"Would you like me to read you a story?" she asked while she was cleaning me up after dinner.

"Yes!" I said shaking my head in vigorous agreement. I tried looking at the book but I couldn't make sense of the words on the page. I recognized certain words but when I tried to identify what they meant, my brain would scatter as if someone had shaken an etch a sketch and I completely lost what I was even trying to figure out. They seemed impossibly big when I looked at words like spaghetti, or marinara. I tried to read those from the containers while my mother was cooking.

She decided to read a book to me that seemed familiar. She came into the room with a glass of milk and some delicious chocolate chip cookies for me. I loved it; they were warm, chewy and gooey and went down great with the glass of fresh, cold, milk.

The story she read to me, was a twisted tale I kept up with about a crazy guy named Sam who wanted this guy to eat some green food to an obsessive degree. He didn't like green food very much though and I think he just wanted to eat the guy's eggs so he would stop asking him.

I asked her to read it to me again to which she smiled and agreed. About halfway through the book the second time I started to get very sleepy. I could see my mother was starting to fall asleep mid-sentence too and before Sam got the guy to eat his green food again, my mother had stopped reading completely. She was fast asleep. *She must have been pretty tired.* I thought. I felt myself drifting uncontrollably to sleep right after.

It wasn't a second more than it took me to lose consciousness when I suddenly felt totally refreshed and awake like I had just woken up from a great night's sleep. I stood up and looked down at the ground where I could see my mother lying there with her head on my chest and her left arm wrapped around my slumped shoulders. I had a string of drool dripping down my chin on my ever so relaxed face and suddenly I felt overwhelmingly sorry for myself as I looked down at my lifeless body. Then it hit me, if I was down there…

I felt a rise of panic as my spiritual heart began beating much too fast. I understood exactly what this meant and I noticed right away that I was able to think more clearly now. My mental deficiencies were wearing off like a fading dream no longer a significant barrier to my thought processes. Almost exactly as I had that thought the fog completely cleared from my muddled mind.

Everything began flooding back to me in waves. It seemed I could relax, that wasn't really me who had just died, it was merely a body that I had stolen. I didn't have the heavy fog of my recent life affecting me like it had the first time I died because I hadn't been in this body for very long. It didn't take much longer before I remembered exactly who I was again and why I was here.

I looked down at the body I thought was my mother until just moments ago and I saw her confused soul begin detaching itself from her physical body. It was like watching Velcro peel apart only instead of the normal Velcro material; it was made from a strong pulsating blue and purple hued light that seemed to have almost invisible membranes holding the two halves together. It reminded me of some sort of 3-d black light animation. She stood up and looked down at her body trying to process what she was seeing. She then lifted her hands in front of her eyes to examine them, probably wondering if any of this was real.

I could actually see the process of acceptance happening all at once, her mouth and eyes widening in unison as she realized this was indeed happening. She then relaxed the features of her spiritual face and looked first down at her dead body and then over at her son's dead body. She appeared to be relieved that she still existed. She slowly examined her son's body lying on the ground. Her features looked so pained; I didn't doubt she was going to do a lot of soul crying. It was different with souls than in a human body. Emotions are felt all over the soul instead of just being a pain in the heart as a human. When a soul cries, it literally shakes like a human body does. She looked so pitiful and yet somehow peaceful at the same time. She put her face into her hands and started to cry. "I'm sorry my son, I couldn't take it that you were so miserable. I couldn't stand there and watch you suffer like that any longer."

She continued weeping for a minute before she realized that someone else was standing there with her and it wasn't her son. She looked at me with blank eyes that seemed to be staring through me instead of at me. I could see she definitely had reached a breaking point in her life.

Even the hair her soul was projecting was tattered and frayed and she had heavy bags under her eyes. She seemed to be so tired although she was made up of limitless energy. It was apparent that her life had exhausted her.

I hadn't noticed before with the muddled mind of her son's body but she was definitely going to be one of those souls that needed to come out of a life and sleep. Some spirits need a form of sleep after an exhausting life. Mostly the ones who lived a life where there was a lot of loss, or subservience to others. There were also those less fortunate who were physically and mentally beaten their entire lives and died a rather violent death. Those ones usually required more sleep than the average soul.

I guess calling it sleep isn't quite accurate. The process is more of a healing or mending of energy, where the tattered and beaten parts of the soul would be replenished with pure energy until it was at a healthy peak again. It was a way to take negative energy and recycle it, turning it into clean repaired good energy. The setup is similar to a sensory deprivation chamber in which you feel no sort of gravity or physicality of any sort. It's like floating on a cloud that pulses a healing energy through a soul in delicious waves, healing any issues that this hell on earth had created.

I hadn't known beforehand but the body I had jumped into was mentally-challenged. It was like playing Russian roulette trying to jump into a body without permission. There was a reason that there were people in charge of things, it seems that humanity and organized systems of superiority aren't limited to only the planet Earth. When you die you realize that there is so much more out there that we didn't know about, at least not on Earth. Sentient thinking beings are everywhere. People might call them a Spirit guide or an Angel even. The truth is there are a lot of different types of beings out there, both in the afterlife and in the physical planes. Only the human ego thinks there couldn't be anything out there that is like or superior to us, because then we wouldn't be so unique.

Chapter 3

I was fully functioning mentally now and I realized that I had just literally lived through being murdered by my own mother. Well, she wasn't really MY mother but I couldn't help but think of her that way. I still had memories in my mind of the way he thought of her and how she seemed to be the lifesaver he had always needed. By killing him she had set him free, or in this case… set me free. She continued to stare at me; she was definitely confused about what was going on.

"Who are you?" she asked me. "Where is my son?"

"I'm sorry ma'am, you seem like a good woman and I'm sure your intentions were justified but that wasn't your son you just killed, it was me. You see, I borrowed your son's body when he left it and I didn't really get to choose where I went because I didn't confer with the Elders."

She looked at me as if I was trying to explain the theory of relativity to her. "What the fuck are you talking about?"

She narrowed her eyes and asked in a more hostile tone. "What have you done with my son… who are you?"

"Listen, your son…" I started to explain but just then she was distracted by a glowing light coming from her right side. I already knew what it was and also knew that she would be too distracted to finish this conversation with me right now. She began walking towards the light forgetting about me completely. "Never mind." I said. "You'll see for yourself soon enough."

She didn't even hear me. She was too busy looking at the bright pulsating warm blue light that suddenly appeared in front of her. It was pulsing slower and slower as it began to align itself with her souls vibrational frequency, which similar to fingerprints is different for everyone else. Finally it pulsed at a steady rhythm and I could see her energy was pulsating at the same speed just on a much smaller scale. The light had matched her frequency and she could now fully see the tunnel entry specific to her life waves and she was mesmerized.

I couldn't see what she was seeing any more than a dull bluish-white glow right now but if I concentrated on changing up my own frequency a bit I could match my energy to hers and see her tunnel as if I had manifested my own out of thin air.

After all that was how this dimension worked. Whatever you wanted to see at any particular time was going to manifest out of nothingness. This was more complicated than that though, as we were on the Earth plane and this was her light. She was about to go to the plane beyond physical existence. The place everybody goes after they die. She was about to go into the afterlife. Everyone gets their own special tunnel attuned to their life waves, even animals. This one however wasn't mine, I was going to have to in a sense, hitchhike.

The last time I had died and been here I had some time to wander the Earth, checking up on loved ones and even seeing how a few old friends I had lost contact with were doing. This time I hadn't exactly died under normal circumstances. I had stolen a body without permission, who knew if they were coming to get me or if a tunnel was even coming for me?

I focused until I could see her tunnel becoming clear to me. The process was much the same as when you adjust a microscope until everything is as high definition as it can get. She was still standing there unsure about jumping into her light, or even how to jump in. I walked past her and showed her how it's done; jumping into her tunnels light while she got up the nerve. I already knew that all of these death tunnels would lead back to the same plane eventually so I wasn't worried about where I would end up.

It was a pretty sweet design how it all worked. When you die; your energy is stuck in a pattern from a lifetime of being inside of a human body. As a human we are at an extremely slow vibration. In fact that's why we have solid matter, the energy is moving so slow that it can't help but become a solid mass. When your soul finds the tunnel, the fog of your life lifts away and your energy vibration gets much higher. The dull glow you would initially see would soon become a beautiful mesmerizing tunnel. As you go through it on your way to the world of the undead your energy is being revitalized with energy from the spiritual plane to make your full self more complete. This process feels like a day at the spa, it's like washing away the dirty humanity that you just shed like a skin of a reptile.

It also doubles as a super highway to the soul realm, a place where people go when they die. Many call it home since it's the place where our actual lives go on between our temporary lives. It's the place where our full consciousness comes into view and we can remember anything and everything we've been through in every life we have ever lived.

Lives are meant for one thing, to experience things so we can further understand them. People on Earth are deluded into believing that we only get one chance to live life and regardless of how it went, due consequence would be meted out for an eternity. Kind of seems like a raw deal for those less fortunate who were born into psychotic families or ways of thinking and never get a chance to lead a heavenly kind of life right? Bullshit. We have good lives and we have bad lives but they are all lived for a purpose. There are legitimate reasons for every life we have ever lived, maybe multiple reasons. The best way to learn something is by experience and what better way to experience everything than by living multiple lives. Those who had lived enough lives are amazing to talk to; they seem to know everything and what's more is they actually understand everything. They are not judgmental; they are understanding and very good at leading someone in a direction to fix their problems. They are sort of like supernatural counselors who are never wrong or give ill advice.

I looked back at her and I could see that my jumping into her light and floating away like I was on a tube in a river eased her mind a little. She climbed in still unsure and quite wobbly, although a nice jump would have worked much better. As a spirit a jump could be infinite, there are literally no limits to what you can do. You simply have to believe its normal the same way you might in a dream. Don't question whether it's real or not or it becomes harder to do what you want since you see it as an obstacle. In this plane, nothing is impossible. She was freshly dead though and hadn't learned any of those tricks yet. She wouldn't remember any of her past lives if she'd had any until she had healed from this life. I knew it would be a while yet until we got back there so I figured I'd just lay back and relax for a while as I thought about my next move.

I suppose that I should explain how I got here. Tell you a little bit about the things that I've been through and why I have been stealing bodies with no regard as to what shape they would be in.

Fair enough. It all started back when I was alive…

About the Author

Mark Lopez was born and raised in the beautiful State of Colorado.

He spends his time writing unmatchable fiction and enjoying the little things life has to offer.

The blood makes it real is the first book in a 3 part series. If you enjoyed this book, then do me a favor and review it for me! Reviews help get my books in front of others to read, freeing up time for me to write more for YOU to enjoy!

As a Self-made author, I need every bit of help that I can get, spreading my word. You can help by:

Telling your friends and other readers about my books and reviewing them for me!

Buying a hard copy version of my books!

Buying the next book in the series Life After Dead!

Subscribing to my site to be updated about future endeavors!

Find me on my website MarkLopezAuthor.com

Find me on twitter @Darkmarklolo

On my Facebook page @DarkMarkLoloAuthor

Email me anytime Darkmarklolo@gmail.com

If you loved this book, Subscribe and be the first to know when my next books come out!

THANK YOU!

Other books by Mark Lopez

Life After Dead

The Art of Death

In A Strangers Eyes

The Creation

Immoral Immortals

Mothers Wrath